STEPHANIE TURNER

Conductor of Crime

Bethany Knox Private Investigator #3

First edition

This book was professionally typeset on Reedsy.
Find out more at reedsy.com

To my David

Contents

1

Man Down

The hotel bar was busy, but not too crowded considering it was a Friday night. The lights were a little bright for my liking, and the jazz band playing on the stage was a little loud, but I wouldn't be staying long; I could tolerate it. I reached up to scratch my forehead under my wig and made myself pull my fingers away. This too shall pass... So I told myself. I wished it would pass faster. I didn't like being in the open like this, and it was making me nervous; I didn't want to be seen.

My target was in place, perched at a table overlooking the room where he could see everyone coming and going, and no one could miss seeing him. I shook my head at that. He'd had a good run, grasping a large chunk of territory from several competitors, making brazen deals with bigger and bigger players as he clawed his way up the food chain, and apparently getting away with it. It had made him cocky. It was about to be his undoing. He stood to shake hands with the man coming to meet him. Target number two: Ryan Valentine.

Valentine was the one we really wanted. He was a small man that always reminded me of a garden gnome, but he was a big fish, and way up that food chain. He was high in the Sept - the largest organized crime gang in Metro. They'd been around for years, but they'd grown over the last decade - in size, reach, and sophistication. They were becoming a problem. Taking Valentine down would scare the other players, keep them in-line, and make them behave. Maybe even make them think twice. That was the theory, anyway, and I was more than willing to help test it.

I pressed the gem on my ring with my finger - the button that controlled the camera in my earring, and took several shots of the men together. I ordered a drink, and swiveled around on my seat, looking around the room like I was looking for someone, like I had a reason to be there, and no interest whatsoever in the goings on of my targets across the room. My gaze came to rest on a table in the center of the room. About a dozen men sat there, drinking and laughing, ties loosened, suit jackets off, blowing off steam after the end of a long and busy work week from the looks of them. The man at the end of the table looked up, his eyes met mine, and held my gaze. Darn it.

I looked away, blushing like a schoolgirl. I swiveled on my seat, and watched in the mirror over the bar as he wended his way across the room toward me. Darn it.

"Have we met before?" From any other man, that would sound trite. From Nigel Essex, scientist and owner of Essex Enterprises, millionaire several dozen times over, with his British accent... He leaned against the bar beside me and ran his finger down the side of my arm, sending a tremor through my entire body. Not fair. "Such soft skin."

"I use the Serenity Skincare line." I tucked a strand of black hair behind my ear and tilted my head, trying to see past his shoulder.

2

"Really?" He smiled broadly, his eyes looked a little glazed; I wondered if he'd had a bit too much to drink. "I developed it." He boasted proudly.

I leaned closer to him and pressed up higher on my seat, trying to get a better view. I put my hand on Nigel's arm to steady myself; his biceps were rock solid. Focus, Bethany! I turned my head so my earring camera was at a better angle, and clicked a shot of the table in the back corner just as Nigel shifted to the right, blocking my view. Darn it! I almost had Valentine!

"I'm certain we've met, but I can't place where." Nigel said.

My heart pounded. His smile broadened, his fingers continued to idly caress my forearm. I'm not sure he was aware of what he was doing. I was very aware; it was not at all unpleasant, and very distracting. "Do you need a hint?"

"Help me out, darling?"

My mouth was quite near Nigel's ear as I whispered. "I'm a nosy, interfering, busybody."

"Bethany!" He reared back in shock.

"Hold still!" I ordered. "You'll ruin my shot." I gave his bicep a little nudge. "Little to the left, please." I took a dozen or so sequential shots of my targets making their trade in full view across the table. "There, I have them!"

And so would my boss - my father, Jake Knox of Opportunity Knox Private Investigators - his van parked just outside to receive my camera feed, and display it to my brother-in-law, Metro Police Sergeant Ray Jensen, in the van with Dad, working a joint operation with us.

Nigel sighed in resignation as he complied, then chuckled sardonically. "My luck."

"Hm?" I murmured.

"I can't get a break with women." Things with Celia Vanderly must not be working out for him; I felt inordinately happy at that thought. "Either they're only interested in my money, or they want whoever it is that's over my shoulder. Who is over my shoulder?"

I sidestepped that question as I slid off my seat. "Maybe you're looking in the wrong place?"

"Obviously." He agreed peevishly. "Everywhere I look I keep seeing you."

"There are worse choices." I laughed sympathetically and bounced up to kiss him on the cheek, but he turned his head. Our lips met.

"Oh, Nigel!" My hand covered my mouth. "I didn't mean to! I'm sorry–"

"I'm not." He slid his arms around me, his mouth lowered towards mine.

I tilted my mouth up to meet his.

"Good work, Beth." Dad's voice came through my com, destroying the moment.

It seemed deliberate.

I pressed my hand to the com in my ear. "You got him? My shots will work?"

"Clear as crystal; we got what we need." My brother-in-law, Ray, replied. "You best clear out. You have about ten seconds till we come in."

"Roger that, over." My eyes met Nigel's; he looked rather deflated. I tugged his tie. "You might want to follow me. Things are about to get... exciting in here."

"My companions..." We looked to the table he'd left; they were quite engrossed with the karaoke machine, and not at all concerned with him. He sighed. "Will probably appreciate the excitement. Lead on."

4

I made a beeline to the front door, Nigel close behind me. We stepped out and to the side as the heavily armed police force streamed by.

Ray clapped me on the shoulder as he passed. "Good work, kiddo."

The officer behind him stopped, glaring at me, and at Nigel. "What the hell are you doing with him?" Officer Jeff Dover. My ex husband.

"Nothing." I blurted.

"It's hardly your business." Nigel said at the same time.

Jeff bristled, his hands balled into fists.

"Dover!" Ray barked. "You with us?"

Jeff ground his teeth and charged inside, but not until after he'd given me a look of pure seething hatred.

Darn it.

I compressed my lips and turned to look up at Nigel. "Sorry about that."

Nigel shook his head. "That was a mistake. This whole night was. Celia is–"

Celia? Darn it. A teal streak shot past us on the road; the color drew my attention. I turned my head, snapping shots of the driver instinctively, not stopping to think why. Then it hit me. "Isn't that your car?"

"Blast it!" Nigel swore as we watched it squeal around the corner.

I tensed. "Where were you parked?"

He pointed with his thumb. "The garage up–"

"Marco!" I ran. Tried to. Stupid heels! I hopped as I ran and tugged them off, then sprinted barefoot towards the garage entrance.

The wooden barricade was smashed, and Marco Firenze was

5

lying on the ground beside it.

"No!" I heard my dress tear as I slid on the pavement to check him. Nigel passed me, and was already on his knees beside him.

Marco groaned, his fingers gripped my arm, then traveled to the welt on his forehead. "What hit me?"

"My car, most likely." Nigel offered irritably. He held a finger in front of Marco's eyes, measuring his tracking. "How many fingers am I holding up?"

"Keep your hand still so I can tell!" Marco snapped at him.

"It is still." Nigel assured him.

Marco groaned, and his eyes rolled up in his head.

"Man down." I barked into my com.

We had a terse exchange, and Ray relayed orders through someone on his end. "Help's on the way, Beth."

"Thank you." I said through my com; I heard gunfire through Ray's in return.

"It's sideways here, kid-"

My com went dead. I pressed my ear frantically. "Ray?"

"What's happening?" Nigel demanded.

"Ray!" I shouted, torn between running to him and staying with Marco.

"Go." Marco made the decision for me.

I turned.

"Beth." Ray's voice came through loud and clear, stopping me in my tracks, resounding with grim satisfaction. "We got them."

"Everyone's OK?" I asked.

Ray didn't answer. Not right away. "Jeff's been shot."

I forgot how to breathe.

The wail of the approaching ambulance siren broke through my stupor.

6

"Bethany." Dad's voice rang loud and clear over my com; as did the note of warning it carried.

I ignored the warning and pulled the com from my ear, left Marco in Nigel's capable hands, and hurtled back the way I'd come.

The captured targets were being loaded into the back of the wagon, and the ambulance pulled up just as I arrived. Jeff walked toward it on his own feet, unaided, holding a gauze pad to his arm and a furious scowl on his face, masking that he was in pain. It was becoming a standard expression.

"Aw, Scarlet's come to kiss you better." Someone said.

Jeff whipped his head around. His eyes met mine. He smiled. Darn it. "What happened?"

"I got shot." He laughed. In shock?

"Jeff."

"Valentine wasn't happy to see me." He smiled. "I'm happy to see you. Alone."

I felt like an idiot. I didn't think. I shouldn't have come. "You're OK?"

"Just a scratch, baby." He reached out for me.

"No!" I stepped back, but he was viper fast; his bloody fingers swirled over my cheek.

"You're still mine."

"I'm still not." I scrubbed at the mark I knew he'd made with my fist: a circle - a serpent devouring itself. The Sept sigil. I felt sick.

Jeff laughed. "See, you keep saying that, but you keep coming back where you belong-"

"I'm not back." I protested. "I don't belong to you."

He smirked at me; his mind was made up. "Then why'd you come?" He asked playfully.

7

"I need intel." I grasped for a reason, any excuse. "Chop shops. High end. Who's active?"

"Who's asking?" Jeff peeled off his shirt, baring his muscles and tattoos, letting the paramedic see to his arm. It was a bit more than a scratch, but it looked like the bullet had gone clean through.

"Essex." I lied. "My client."

"That's why you were with him." Jeff's smile broadened, relieved, grasping after his own reasons. Darn it. This was backfiring, making it worse, giving him hope. "Check Lakeside first, then Albro Terrace."

"Pope's active?"

"Can't keep a good man down. Make sure you say hi for me." He told me what I needed to know, but he was handing out orders like I was on his team, working under him again. "Just like old times." He said. "I knew you'd come back to me."

Darn it.

2

Back and Forth

I made my way back to the garage, feeling a bit like a yo-yo flinging back and forth. I wondered who was controlling my string, because it sure wasn't me.

The paramedics were with Marco, loading him onto a stretcher. He was barely protesting; that wasn't a good sign.

"You should know better!" Dad intercepted me. "Ray should know better! Why-"

"Habit?" I shrugged. "I was with him for seven years; I can't just turn that off-"

"Learn how!" Dad snapped. "Jeff's lost any right to your concern-"

"I've got a job." I deflected.

"You need to decompress." He argued.

"I decompress by moving, and I need to move fast on this-"

"On what?"

"Dr. Essex's car." I said; Nigel's head snapped up when he heard his name, and he approached. "I've got two leads-"

"Where?" Dad demanded.

"Lakeside, and Albro Terrace-"

9

"Pope's active?"

"Jeff said he was."

"He'd know." Dad sighed. "I hate to leave Marco-"

"Don't." I said. "He'll feel better if you're there; it's probably the only way he'll stay for treatment."

Dad narrowed his eyes at me, but he couldn't argue my logic. "You can't go alone-"

"I'll go with her." Nigel volunteered; my heart started to pound.

"I'm sure your insurance will cover the car." Dad argued.

"It's the principle." Nigel argued back. "I'm fond of that car, and I don't like having my things taken without my permission. If Bethany has found a trail, then I'd like to follow it."

Dad pursed his lips. "This is getting to be a habit. You considering a career change?"

"Just might." Nigel grinned.

"Just be careful." Dad told me.

"I will." I promised.

"I'll make sure of it." Nigel added.

I glared at him before I could stop myself; his grin broadened.

Dad clapped him on the shoulder. "Good man."

"I try." Nigel nodded.

I frowned. "This way."

Nigel fell in beside me as we went up the road to where I'd parked my van. I pulled bobby pins from my wig as we walked, and ripped it off the second we ducked inside my stealth living quarters, shaking free my red hair. The wig landed on the counter, my earrings were plugged into my laptop, and the images I'd shot with them began downloading.

"Wait up front." I pointed Nigel to the cab.

He shook his head no. "Your father was right; my interest's

been piqued. I'd like to see how you work."

"You're not seeing how I change."

His face colored. "I'll just wait up front, then. Shall I drive?"

I winced; I hadn't meant to be so abrupt. Side effects of Jeff? "Do you know where Albro Terrace is?" Jeff had said Lakeside first, but Albro was closer, and I had a hunch...

"Across the bridge, or the back way?"

"Back way." I tossed him the keys.

Nigel started the van, and I started to change. Heels and dress were exchanged for runners, pants, and shirt; all black, my new standard these days. I sat on the banquette to tie up my shoes, so I didn't go flying too far when the van lurched and thumped over something in the road.

"What was that?" I shouted.

"Just a homeless person." Nigel called back. "Don't think he caused too much damage-"

"What!?" I sprinted for the cab.

"I hit the curb." Nigel laughed deprecatingly, trying to cover his embarrassment. "I'm accustomed to a tighter turn radius."

"Oh, good grief." I rubbed my temples. "How much did you have to drink?"

"Not very much." He sounded offended.

"Maybe I should-"

"I'm quite capable to drive." Nigel said archly. "This thing's rather sluggish."

"It's built for stealth, not for speed." I said defensively. "It does its job well." I patted the dash so its feelings wouldn't be hurt.

Nigel rolled his eyes.

I ignored that, and took advantage of having my hands free to grab my laptop while he drove. My earrings finished their

11

download, and I scrolled through the images until I found one with a clear picture of the kid driving Nigel's car. Clear-ish. He'd been traveling fast, and there were a lot of reflection's on the window so none of them were great. I forwarded the best of the lot to my sister, Hailey, to clean up and see what she could find on the driver; that was her thing. I had other strengths.

I pulled out my phone, and called my brother. We'd both known Evan Pope since kindergarten, and Johnny counted him a friend. They were both mechanics, and also, sometimes racers. Their world's had frequently crossed.

"Beth?" He answered his phone.

"Johnny; I'm on my way to Albro Terrace-"

"I heard Pope was out of jail," He confirmed what Jeff said; Johnny raced his cars on a track; Pope ran the tracks, but he also took his cars on the street, and his cars weren't always his. That's what had got him thrown into jail the last time. "And right back up to his old tricks."

Sounds like he hadn't learned. "Nice of you to let me know-"

"I just heard," Johnny said defensively. "If you came to Sunday dinner-"

"Not happening." I said instantly. "Not yet." I qualified, softening my tone, feeling guilty, and only about to add to it. "Jeff was shot-"

"What?" Johnny demanded.

Nigel looked at me sharply, then turned his eyes back to the road.

I sank deeper into my seat. "It was only a flesh wound." Johnny didn't laugh the way I'd hoped he would; even though we'd split apart, Jeff was still one of his best friends. I tried to deflect. "I'm more concerned about Marco-"

"What happened to Marco?"

"Concussion; Nigel's car hit him–"

"Who's Nigel?"

"Dr. Essex." I winced. "He wasn't driving–"

"Who was?"

"I don't know. I sent pics of the guy to Hailey; can you have a look and see if you recognize him?"

"I'll look." Johnny said. "After I stop by the hospital." He hung up.

I sighed, wondering what my strengths were. They seemed to have deserted me.

"That's where you ran off to, then?" Nigel asked. "Your ex was hurt?"

I bristled defensively. "He'll be fine."

"You seem to have a complicated relationship."

"Yes." I deflated. "Complicated." I didn't want to discuss it. "What kind of system did you have on your car?"

"System?"

"Security? GPS? Any chance of a built-in tracker?"

"No chance at all." Nigel said. "I deliberately avoided one."

"Why?"

"I prefer to avoid being a target."

"Target for what?"

"I have rather a lot of money," He smirked. "And there are people that feel entitled to try and take what I've earned for themselves; I try not to make it easy for them to find me. Most tracker's are all too easy to hack."

"True, that." I sighed. "But it would have made it easier to find your car."

"But where'd be the fun in that?" Nigel asked sarcastically.

I laughed. "Turn in here." I directed Nigel as I closed up my laptop and got my head in gear. "Park in the loading zone; I won't be long."

"What's our game plan?" Nigel asked.

"The game plan is I go in, you wait in the van-"

"No."

"What do you mean, no? I have a job to do-"

"And I'm bankrolling it." Nigel reminded me. "I want in on it."

I rubbed my temple. "Would you let just anyone come in off the street and start mixing chemicals in one of your labs?"

"I'm not just anyone off the street-"

"You're not trained-"

"I am eminently trained!" Nigel reared back, deeply offended. "My money makes me a target; I have to know how to read a situation and take care of my own safety-"

"This is more than that-"

"In what way?" He demanded.

"We don't have time for a philosophy lesson! If you want me to find your car-"

He changed tactics. "I swore to your father that I would keep you safe. I have to be at your side to do that. Would you have me break my word?"

"Really? You're going to play the guilt card?"

"Oh, I'm utterly shameless." His smile proved it; I'd never seen a man so pleased with himself, and so certain he was going to have his way.

I bit my cheek to keep in the retort I wanted to make. It doesn't do to swear at a paying customer.

"And I'm very attached to that car-"

"Boys and their toys." I snarked.

"It was the last gift my grandfather gave to me before he died." Nigel's voice was acid, but his eyes were blazing with anger, and with grief. "It's not just a car, it's my last link with him. No one else has a right to it. I have to find it. I have to at least try to help."

Darn it. He was human after all.

I sighed. "Wait here." I held up my hand to stop the forming protest. "A change in plans requires a change in outfit."

3

Change in Plans

I slipped between the seats and shut the door, muttering to myself about how bad of an idea this was, and what a sucker I was; Nigel's eyes had done me in. Show me an injured animal or a person in distress, and I became putty. I suppose there were worse things.

I whipped off the black, and tugged my way into a clingy red spandex and sequin dress that left little to the imagination. My comfy sneakers were replaced with stilettos I definitely could not run in. I pulled out my brightest red lipstick, and went to town with it. Private Investigator Rule #1: Don't draw attention, blend in with your surroundings; I would fit in perfectly in this get up. I turned and saw myself in the full length mirror attached to the cabin door. I looked like a cheap hooker. Jeff would have loved it. I hated it.

"I'm not his anymore." I told my reflection.

I pulled the red dress off over my head, and replaced it with the black cocktail dress I had on earlier. The inner lining had torn when I slid to help Marco, but it wasn't noticeable from the outside. There was probably a metaphor in there, but I didn't want to look for it.

The dress was elegantly form fitting with just a little bit of swing to the hem, and it felt like a suit of armor compared to the red number. I'd spent more time than I'd meant to changing, so the stilettos remained. I quickly opened my make-up bag, toned down my lips, and played up my eyes. A flash of silver in the bottom of my bag caught my attention, a necklace I'd thought I'd thrown away, the pendant a silver circle - a snake eating its own tail: the Sept sigil. It made my skin crawl, but it would ease my way through the door. I put it on.

I flicked on my rooftop camera to see outside; the coast was clear. I opened the door to the cab. "Ready?"

"Never more." Nigel followed me through the sliding door on the side of the van.

"Stay close to me - but don't touch me, and mind what you say; it's probably better if you don't say anything." I warned him. "Don't let yourself be goaded into a fight."

He looked at me with a rather dubious expression. "Where are we headed, exactly?"

"The first level of Hell."

"Is that all?" He quipped. I couldn't decide if he was being playful or defensive. "Have we far to go?"

"We're here." I knocked on the black steel door in what looked like a fairly non-descript brick warehouse.

A window in the door slid open; a bouncer I didn't recognize looked me up and down. "What do you want?"

I held up the necklace and didn't say a word.

The door opened, and we went in.

"Who's he?" The bouncer asked.

I frowned at Nigel. "My bodyguard."

Nigel grinned.

The bouncer eyed Nigel askance, then shrugged. "Go on." He shut the door and buzzed us in.

I took a deep breath, then opened the second door. The music hit me like a physical blast. The place was darker than I liked, and crammed from end to end with bodies flailing about in what was supposed to be dancing but looked to me more like epileptic seizures. I made sure Nigel was with me, then led him quickly along the edge of the room, around the corner, and down the stairs. We went through a third door. The music was still audible, but blessedly muffled behind us. Our shoes clacked on the black tiles in the corridor.

"This seems a strange place to hide a car." Nigel said.

I agreed with that estimation. "It's a strange place."

We quickly passed the bathroom where someone was being sick, and I checked the pulse of a guy lying passed out on the floor in a doorway; it was strong, breathing was regular; we kept going. We walked on to the point where the hallway branched; the coast was clear. We went up a short flight of stairs and I pushed open door number four.

"What the hell are you doing here?" Sage demanded.

"None of your business." I told him, and moved for door number five.

His ample body blocked my way. "You don't got no business here."

"Dove sent me here."

Sage crossed his arms, disbelieving.

"Open up." I ordered.

He didn't budge. Darn it.

"What the hell are you doing here?" Spider snarled, coming through the door behind me.

"That's getting repetitive." Nigel remarked, and was ignored.

18

Spider was laser focused on me. "Jeff told you Lakeside first-"

"So you'd have time to get here and move the car before I could find it?"

"So you wouldn't have to come here at all!" His words said one thing, but his scowl told me I'd hit pay dirt. "He was trying to protect you! You never deserved him."

I crossed my arms tight around my middle. Spider was a master at wielding words into weapons, stabbing you with sharp bits of the truth, but he never told the whole truth. "I never deserved to be treated-"

"You got what you deserved." He snarled. "Better than you deserved."

I looked away, my face hot with shame and fury. "Open it." I barked at Sage.

He looked to Spider for direction; Spider didn't look pleased, but he nodded permission. Sage shuffled desultorily aside. Almost. "Who's he?" He nodded at Nigel with three of his chins.

"None of your business." I repeated.

He scowled, but pushed the button that released the door, and sat back on his stool. I was surprised it held him.

Spider led the way, walking so fast it was hard for me to keep up with him in my heels. The music cut off completely when the door closed behind us. Door number six loomed ahead; we turned sharply, avoiding it altogether. That was fine with me; I never wanted to go through it again. I walked faster, wanting to be away from this place as quickly as I could. We came to the end of the hall.

Spider pushed open the steel door, flicked on the over-head florescent lights, and crossed his arms, smiling smugly. "Should've gone to Lakeside."

I stepped onto the metal grating beside him and looked down

19

at the shop floor. Every single bay was full; none of them held anything resembling Nigel's car. My phone rang.

"Hailey," I smiled as I took my sister's call. "How's Lakeside?"

Spider scowled.

"Nothing doing." She said; I heard a beep as the picture I'd sent her came back to me - far clearer, but the identity of our thief still remained a mystery to me. "I'm still running him; InSight's boggy as usual. Want me to ask around here, see if anyone recognizes him?"

"I'd appreciate it."

"I'll call if I find anything." She hung up.

I smiled sweetly at Spider. "Recognize him?" I showed him the image on my phone.

He glanced at it, and shook his head no. "Not our crew. Don't know him."

Darn it. I believed him; at least that our mystery man wasn't a play mate. That Spider didn't know him at all? I suppose it was possible, but it just didn't seem likely. His web stretched too far, and reached into too many corners for him not to know. "Where else could the car be?"

"How would I know?" He snarled, and shoved me aside to get to the door.

"You wouldn't without Jeff to tell you." I snapped at him, and instantly regretted it.

"You watch your mouth." He rounded on me, looming over me and doing his best to look intimidating. He didn't have to try very hard. "You wouldn't dare talk to me like that if he were here-"

"He isn't here," Nigel pushed in front of me. "But I am, and I will not stand to hear her spoken to in that manner."

Spider laughed in his face. "Back off before you get hurt, British."

I put a hand on Nigel's arm to restrain him.

Nigel glared at Spider but backed up, staying between him and me.

Spider laughed, and went back through the door.

I wanted to find Pope, but I didn't want to go back through the maze, so I directed Nigel down the stairs onto the shop floor. "You're lucky."

"What? That that goon didn't tempt his luck?"

I shook my head at him, not wanting to argue. I just wanted out of here. "Come on."

"Do the police know of this place?" Nigel asked.

"Spider's a cop." I laughed at his expression.

"I recall him now... I didn't recognize him without the uniform. Charming fellow." He repressed a shudder. "He seems to fit in quite well here."

"He keeps an eye on the activity here." I said. "But he rarely does anything about it. Most of the business is legit, and as long as the stuff that isn't keeps a low profile..." I shrugged. "It's usually more trouble than it's worth to bother about."

Nigel was not impressed. "Our tax dollars at work."

"You get what you pay for." I retorted. "Policing isn't given high priority in the city budget, so we have to prioritize what offenders and which offenses merit our attention."

"We?" Nigel picked that up right away.

"I spent seven years on the force. Old habits die hard."

We went out through the shop door. It locked behind us automatically, sealing us out with a click. I led the way through a dim alley toward the van.

"Where next?" Nigel asked. "Do you have more ideas?"

"A few. They may be long shots–"

"I'm willing to take them."

"You're persistent."

"I want my car back, and I don't like to quit."

"Good." I respected that. "There are two places nearby I want to check out, and one a bit off the beaten path."

We turned the corner and came to the lot with my van. A man was leaning against the door, smoking a cigarette, waiting for me. Evan Pope. Just the man I wanted to see.

"You're a sight for sore eyes, Red." Pope hugged me with one arm.

"I was hoping to lay eyes on you." I returned the hug with both arms.

"Can't always get what you want." He grinned.

"I get what I can." I passed him my phone, our mystery man's pic on display. "Do you know him?"

Pope whistled. "You don't want to know him."

"No." I agreed. "I just want to recover the car he stole tonight."

"My advice; let it go."

"Not happening." I said before Nigel could respond. "Who is he, and where do I find him?"

"He's Jimmy Maestro's nephew, Angelo." Pope watched my reaction carefully, grinning at what he saw.

I was ticked; there's no way Spider hadn't known who he was.

"Who's Jimmy Maestro?" Nigel asked.

"Who's he?" Pope pointed to Nigel with his cigarette.

"My client." I said.

"And you brought him here?" Pope laughed incredulously. "Dove know?"

"He sent me."

22

"Sent you out of the way." Pope shook his head.

I couldn't disagree, and I wasn't happy about it. "Where should he have sent me?"

Pope shrugged.

I rephrased my question. "Where do I find Maestro?"

"Where's Dove?" Pope dragged on his cigarette, not answering me.

"Hospital," I said; Pope raised an eyebrow. "He got shot earlier tonight."

"Bad?"

"Flesh wound." I shook my head. "He's probably out already."

"Can't keep a good man down." Pope grinned wolfishly. "How's Hailey?"

"Good," I said. "She's married, third kid on the way."

"What?" He frowned. "Married?"

"As far as your concerned, she might as well be. My sister's off limits. Where do I find Maestro?"

Pope laughed. "You're not getting something for nothing. How 'bout you give me Hailey's number?"

"You tell me," I bargained. "You get to keep your teeth."

"You got a big mouth, little girl."

"I can back up what I say," I smiled sweetly. "And you know it."

"You can go to hell." Pope flung his cigarette on the ground and stubbed it with his heel, angry and embarrassed by the reminder.

Nigel blocked him from leaving. "The lady asked you a question."

Pope looked Nigel up and down, and must have figured it wasn't worth the effort to resist. "Your funeral." He shrugged

23

like he didn't care. "Try the Grotto."

"At Newell Lake?" Nigel was shocked.

"Can't promise he's there, but someone there will know where to find him." Pope said. "I didn't tell you."

I nodded assurance. "I'm silent as the grave."

"Not with that mouth." He snorted a laugh, then his expression changed. "Tell Hailey I'm sorry."

I compressed my lips. "I will. Stay out of trouble, Evan."

"Not likely." He said, and headed for the door to Hell.

I felt sick inside watching him go, but I shoved it down. It was his life, his choice. I hoped it wouldn't lead to his funeral.

"I'm lucky?" Nigel looked askance at me. "Do you always threaten people's dental work?"

"Just his." I laughed. "I accidentally hit him in the mouth with a volleyball, and he lost his two front teeth. The day before senior prom."

"Ouch." Nigel said.

"I don't know why he's still upset about it; his team won."

Nigel laughed, and held up my keys. "Newell Lake, then?"

"Fast as we can."

Nigel frowned at my van but refrained from comment.

He was a smart man.

4

A Spot of Bother

"Who's this Maestro chap?" Nigel asked as he drove up the high-way towards Newell Lake and the high class Italian restaurant, Grotto.

"Trouble." I said. "He started out as a small time drug dealer, but he's got his fingers into every sort of organized crime you can think of now. At least that's what we think. He's proven smart and careful, and hard to pin down. There's always a buffer between him and everyone we suspect works for him, and no one will turn on him. Snitching tends to rapidly decrease a person's lifespan."

"So he's a mob boss?"

"Essentially."

"And the nephew?"

"I've never heard of him before, but the Maestro family were never in my territory when I was on the force." I was grateful for that; the Sept had been more than enough to deal with.

"I don't like that he's so close to my territory." Nigel frowned as we took the turnoff that went past his lab. "Grotto caters most of our large events. It's a favorite among much of my staff; I don't want trouble landing on them-"

"It's not likely." I tried to reassure him. "From the little I know of Maestro he doesn't like to mix business and pleasure, or business and business. He doesn't work where he eats, and he works hard to keep the legit stuff squeaky clean."

Nigel didn't look appeased. He turned into the lot and drove for the front of the restaurant.

"If you park around back, my van will blend-"

"If I have to go in, I prefer to make an entrance." Nigel said, and pulled up in front of the valet.

"Oh, good grief." I quickly pulled all my valuable electronic equipment from the cab and slid it through the door to my living quarters, then locked the door between the seats. I reached for my door handle.

"Ah," Nigel tsked. "Wait."

"Why?"

"It's how proper ladies behave." He grinned as I glared at him.

Nigel walked around the front of the van and opened my door for me. He helped me down, took my arm, and handed my van key to the rather dubious looking attendant. "Treat her well." Nigel patted the door, and passed the attendant a large tip.

"Yes, Sir." The attendant smiled broadly and made a hopping bow before driving away with my home.

We walked up the steps, and into a crowded and dimly lit waiting area where a couple were arguing with the concierge. Loudly.

"We've been waiting almost two hours for a table!" The woman was irate. "Tell him, Lloyd." She poked her date in the ribs.

Lloyd spread his hands in helpless entreaty.

"I'm sorry, Sir." The concierge calmly addressed her harassed date. "Every table is currently spoken for, as is every seat in the lounge." Darn it; that made our plan more difficult. "You may continue to wait here, if you so choose." His sniff indicated what he thought of that idea.

Nigel cleared his throat.

The concierge tilted his head with a flicker of annoyance in his direction, but his eyes widened and his manner altered distinctly when he recognized who it was. "Dr. Essex! How may I serve you, Sir?"

"It's a pity you're full-"

"I'm sure we can find a table for you, wherever you like."

Nigel smiled benevolently; Lloyd's date looked like she was about to turn apoplectic. Nigel's eyes widened in recognition. "I know your face, but I don't believe we're acquainted; your name?"

"Frederic, Sir." The concierge gave a worried little bow.

"I believe your box is across from mine at the Trident."

Frederic nodded, looking relieved. "Season's tickets - more my wife's idea than mine, but if it keeps her happy." He shrugged.

"That's always the goal." Nigel kissed my hand.

"Always." Frederic gave a knowing nod of his head.

"Frederic, could you tell me if a Mr. Maestro is in attendance this evening?"

Frederic swallowed audibly. "I do believe he is, Sir."

"Inform him I'd like a word." Nigel passed Frederic a crisp $100 bill. "At his earliest convenience."

"Immediately, Sir." Frederic smiled broadly, bowing again. "Would you care to wait in the lounge while a table is prepared?"

27

Lloyd's date fainted.

"That would be excellent, thank you, Frederic."

We were escorted to the bar, and attended at warp speed by the staff there. It seemed there were some perks to having Nigel's assistance. We had just received our drinks when Frederic returned.

"Mr. Maestro will receive you now, if it please you?"

"It does." Nigel took my arm, and we followed our concierge up a roped-off spiral staircase toward a dim corner of a private balcony where it was easy to see, but not be seen. I respected that. The man seated at the table leaned a little into the light and I gasped.

"What is it?" Nigel asked softly.

"That's not Angelo." I whispered.

The man at the table was older, dark haired, and made of compacted muscle over a stocky frame. His eyes were close-set and shrewd, watching everything, missing nothing.

"That's Jimmy."

"Good." Nigel grinned. "I prefer to dine with the adults."

I nearly turned apoplectic, but we'd reached the table and Jimmy Maestro stood, gesturing for us to sit in his booth.

"Dr. Essex," Maestro bowed his head to Nigel, and gave me only a cursory and rather dismissive look, as if I were little more than a piece of furniture. "Welcome to my establishment."

"Yours?" Nigel asked.

"I own this section of the business park," Maestro smiled; it was an almost pleasant expression, and one I didn't think he used often. "And I appreciate the business your company has so frequently brought to it."

"We have appreciated your hospitality." Nigel took my fingers in his, and Maestro seemed to notice me for the first time, but I wasn't sure I liked his attention. His gaze was disconcerting; I felt weighed, measured, and diced to pieces by his inspection, and was relieved when he turned back to Nigel. "I do hope the relationship can continue."

Maestro's eyes narrowed suddenly, locked on my throat.

I reached up nervously, and nearly fainted; I'd forgotten to remove my necklace. Darn it.

"What brings you to my table?" Maestro turned his gaze back to Nigel, his manner turned cool and guarded.

"A spot of bother," Nigel nudged me, and I passed my phone to Maestro.

His bodyguard stepped in, taking the phone from me and checking it over; his eyes widened when he saw the photo on the display, but he quickly schooled his features before handing it to his boss. Maestro's expression altered when he saw the display; he was angry, and it was a look I never wanted to see again. His eyes flicked to me, and back to Nigel.

"Your nephew has... borrowed my car without my permission." Nigel's tone was as cool as Maestro's. "I should like it returned. Immediately."

"Dr. Essex, I am embarrassed by this unfortunate misunderstanding." Sweat beaded on Maestro's forehead. He whipped out a handkerchief, dabbing at his face. Jimmy Maestro was nervous? His eyes flickered from Nigel to me again. Not me - my necklace. Darn it. "My nephew, he's a headstrong boy-"

"He rather needs to be taken in hand." Nigel said acidly.

Maestro paled, and stood, holding his hand to his heart; I nearly had a heart attack. "Please, I will do what I need to do - anything in my power to maintain good relations. My table is yours for the evening, and any time you wish it. Your car will be at the front door by the time your meal is finished, compliments

29

of the house." His eyes flicked to me again. Was he holding his breath?

I bowed my head nervously, not liking his attention so intensely fixed on me; Maestro exhaled audibly.

Nigel smiled. "So glad we could come to a reasonable arrangement like civilized gentlemen."

"Please, enjoy your evening." Maestro wiped his forehead and gave a small bow; he looked relieved. "A mistake like this will never happen again."

"Say no more about it." Nigel waved away his apology. "We're all friends here." He extended his hand; Maestro looked taken aback, then stepped in and shook it.

"I'm very pleased to hear it." Maestro gave his terrifying smile again, bowed to me, and walked away, his bodyguards falling into place around him.

"Well," Nigel smiled happily. "That went even better than expected."

I couldn't get my necklace off fast enough. I threw it on the table, breathing hard, holding my head in my hands, trying to figure out what to do.

"Bethany?" Nigel asked. "What is it?"

"It's not good." I gasped in a breath, trying not to hyperventilate. "It's really not good."

5

Dabbler in Paranoia

Nigel was positively enjoying himself. "You're saying I inadvertently brokered a deal with a crime boss?" He laughed at the idea, and took another bite of his lobster.

I could have kicked him for not taking this seriously, but our resident concierge arrived to check on the progress of our meal.

"Madam is not eating?" Frederic noted with a great deal of concern. "Is it not-"

"It is wonderful." I did my best to smile; he looked relieved, but stood, watching me, waiting for proof. I took a bite; it tasted a little strongly of garlic for my liking, but I smiled to show I was satisfied. He bowed himself away.

"It is very good, isn't it?" Nigel said. "And the service has been so accommodating. I rarely dine out, but I might have to come here more often."

"Nigel-"

"Bethany, I'm sure you're over-reacting."

I narrowed my eyes at him.

He winced, and made a desperate stab at recovery: "Please, tell me again what you think I've done wrong."

"You're mocking me."

"I'm British. I can't help it. Part of my heritage or some such."

I couldn't help laughing; he grinned, proud of himself. "It wasn't anything you've done, it was how Maestro took it, and how I influenced him." I poked at the necklace.

Nigel noticed, and reached for it.

I let out a strangled squeak of protest and his hand froze, then moved away. I relaxed. Marginally.

"What is it?"

"Trouble." I said. "It's the Sept's sigil-"

"Sept?" Nigel made a sharp intake of breath. "The street gang?"

"Street gang?" I shook my head at that. "They're practically a cult."

"I thought they were defunct?"

"Hardly." I laughed bitterly. "That was their clubhouse we went to earlier. One of them."

Nigel's eyes widened, then narrowed. "That explains a few things."

I shrugged helplessly. "They've learned to be more discreet than they used to be, but they've never gone away. They're embedded into so many things."

"Vanderly's of the underworld?" Nigel asked teasingly.

"They might as well be." I couldn't laugh.

"How were you involved with them?"

"No woman is Sept." I recited by rote Jeff's favorite maxim to shut me out and cut me off from anything he didn't want to tell me. "I was no exception. But I was close enough on the fringes to see in."

"Jeff." Nigel made the connection. "He used to belong. Or he still does?"

"It's complicated."

"In what way?"

"They don't like to let go." They taught Jeff well, I thought to myself. "He's not with them anymore, not like he was, but they won't let him walk away entirely. They keep finding ways to drag him back."

"He must be useful to them in his current profession." Nigel reasoned. "Keeping them informed?"

"Selectively." I closed my eyes tight. "He doesn't have a choice."

"We always have a choice." Nigel countered.

"It's not always a good choice."

He didn't argue the point. "And the trouble with Maestro is... "

"Competition. Maestro and the Sept have unspoken bound-aries worked out across most of Metro, and they don't stray into each other's territory. New areas are tricky until the boundaries have been established. Newell Lake is a prize they both would want."

"You're assuming-"

"It's not a hard assumption to make. It's a logical conclusion; whoever holds it gets easy access by sea and by land with little oversight for their products, and they can bury themselves in amongst respectable businesses-"

"Mixing legal and illegal activities? I thought Maestro doesn't work where he eats?"

"Maestro doesn't, at least he hasn't, but the Sept doesn't make that distinction. They consider themselves respectable business owners, only some of that business has more govern-ment approval than others. It's easier to hide in the muddle, and it makes it easier to keep off the police radar. It legitimizes them."

"I suppose that makes a sort of sense." Nigel frowned. "So what's the issue?"

"You made peace with Maestro; you offered friendship, and shook hands."

"So?"

"So you just ceded the territory, and Sept doesn't share."

"But I'm not Sept."

"But Maestro thinks you are."

"Because of the necklace you wore?"

"It's a brazen declaration to wear it." I cringed at the venomous thing lying on the table. "Only the top tier in the organization are allowed to own the silver; they're not allowed to flaunt it, but they're allowed to decorate their favorite possession with it."

"Possession?" Nigel's eyebrows climbed at that.

"No woman is Sept." I shrugged. "They're not exactly high on feminism and equal rights."

"And Jeff is top tier?"

"Not exactly..."

"Not exactly?"

"Nowhere near." I admitted. "But he was a lot nearer than you. When the Sept hear of this, they'll come for me, and they'll come for you, and not because of your money."

"And I suppose Maestro might have a similar reaction?"

"Very likely."

"How would they even find out?"

"They always find out."

"Darling," Nigel took my hands in his and smiled in a manner that just narrowly avoided being patronizing. "The Sept would have no reason to care, not about my car or our dinner activities.

They would have no reason to look. As for Maestro, my company provides his legitimate business with a lot of business; he simply can't afford to lose me as a customer. I'm sure that was Maestro's chief and only concern."

"I'm not."

"Should I test our food for arsenic?" Nigel asked, teasing me.

His grin took the edge off my paranoia and I deflated a little, realizing how ridiculous I must sound, even to myself. I was probably imagining things. I'll keep telling myself that.

"Acute lead poisoning would be more his style." I told Nigel.

"Harder to hide, though." Nigel posited. "The taste gives it away."

"More the sound, not to mention the blood." I argued; he looked confused. "Bullet wounds tend to be fairly obvious."

"Ah, that type of lead poisoning."

"What does arsenic taste like?" I wondered.

"Metallic, a bit garlicky." He dabbed his finger in my sauce, testing it, then shrugged. "I think we're safe."

"Do you know this from experience? Taste testing chemicals at work?"

He laughed. "I'm not a dabbler in poisons as a rule; I've simply read too much Agatha and Arthur."

"I don't think that's possible."

"No?" He grinned. "You read the great detectives? I thought you favored Victor Powell?"

"I enjoy his books," I said carefully, working to keep my expression neutral. "But once I've read them, I have no desire to re-read them. He doesn't command a lot of staying power."

"Are you still seeing him?" Nigel asked point blank.

"Not exclusively." I said lamely, wishing I could say no, and cursing myself for agreeing to give Victor another chance.

Nigel pursed his lips, and given his expression, I braced myself for a withering rebuff. "Then are you free tomorrow night? There's a Monteverdi concert at the Trident-"

"L'Orfeo?"

"Yes," Nigel grasped my fingers in his. "It's my favorite."

"Mine too."

His smile broadened. "I'd enjoy your company."

My heart soared up, then crashed down with a thud. Darn it. "My evening is booked."

Nigel's face fell, and he let go my fingers. "You're going with Victor?"

I winced. "Sorry."

"I need to stop waiting till the last minute."

"My afternoon is free..." I offered.

"Mine is not." He wrinkled his nose. "Breakfast?"

"That will work." I laughed, and nodded my head eagerly. "Cove Bakery?"

"Boardwalk side." Nigel smiled. "Is nine too early?"

"Nine will work." My heart fluttered. "Nine's perfect."

6

Bracing for Impact

I woke before dawn and went for my morning run. The air was sticky and muggy; it felt like a storm was brewing. I looked to the sky and willed it to stay clear until after my breakfast date with Nigel. I finished warming up around the pond, then pushed full tilt up the hill, reaching the cliff just as the sun tried to crest the horizon. The thick clouds billowing in the distance were an unhealthy purple-bruise color that blocked out the sun, and did not leave much room for optimism regarding the strength of my will. I reversed the process down the hill, stopped at the playground to do my pull-ups on the monkey bars, and headed back to my van.

The lights were off inside my best friend Evie's house so I let her sleep. I completed my ablutions in my van, and debated eating a little something now, or waiting till nine when I was to meet Nigel. I opted for a cup of tea, opened my back doors wide to the morning, and settled onto my tummy to read on the bed. My brain wouldn't cooperate, the words on the pages swimming about uselessly without their meaning penetrating; the combination of excitement about my upcoming date with

Nigel and worry about the possible fallout from last night's meeting with Maestro kept my internal hamster wheel spinning at full speed. I felt nervous and restless and couldn't keep still, so I changed my clothes. Three times. I finally settled on a sky-blue sun dress, and sneaked into Evie's back porch to borrow her white leather sandals, hoping if I dressed for a sunny day the sun might cooperate, all while stubbornly ignoring the darkening sky.

A police squad car whipped into the driveway while I was crossing back from Evie's porch to my van, freezing me in its headlights. The engine revved and I closed my eyes tight, bracing for impact.

It didn't come.

The engine cut off and I opened my eyes to see the car had stopped inches from my shin. Jeff and Spider stepped out of the car, laughing at me.

"Aw, did I spook you, Scarlet?" Spider cackled, and planted himself between me and Evie's door.

I did my best to ignore him. "How's your arm?" I asked Jeff.

"Stings like blazes." He turned his puppy dog eyes on me. "You want to kiss me better?"

I crossed my arms and ignored that, too. "They let you work today?"

"We're short staff." Jeff crossed his arms, mirroring me. Deliberately. "And I need the overtime." That sounded like an accusation; he missed having my salary in our formerly shared bank account. Too bad for him. "Besides, Valentine's on the street," Jeff shrugged, and leaned against my van. "I might as well be, too."

My heart started to pound; they'd cut off my exits. They'd done it so casually, almost naturally. Almost. I knew them too well. Jeff's words sank in. "They let Valentine go?"

"Didn't even stay the night." Spider snarled.

"What's the point in doing a job that doesn't stay done?" Jeff asked. "Try to do the right thing, try to make a difference, risk your life for it," He smacked the bandage on his arm. "And for what?"

I knew better than to answer that. "What brings you by?" I asked as evenly as I could, backing up slowly, keeping them both in my field of view, fighting the urge to bolt.

"You." Jeff smiled.

I had to work not to dig my nails into my palms. "What, really?"

"Angelo Maestro's been found dead." Jeff cut to the chase.

"Murdered?" I asked; he nodded.

"After you were seen waving his picture about." Spider put in.

"You didn't tell me who he was." I reminded him.

"Who did?" Jeff asked.

"Why does it matter?" I asked.

"It matters." Spider said.

"To who?" I asked.

"Who told you?" Jeff demanded.

"Where was he found?" I asked instead. "How did he-"

"What do you know, Beth?" Jeff over-rode me.

I compressed my lips.

"You see him last night?" Spider demanded.

"Speak to him?" Jeff asked.

I felt like the ball in a tennis match, bounced back and forth between them, deliberately kept off balance by their rapid barrage of questions. "The only time I saw him was when I snapped that picture. I didn't know who he was then-"

"When did you find out?" Spider stabbed to the heart. "I

didn't tell you. Who did?"

"Why do you think someone told me?" I countered.

"Essex got his car back." Jeff took a step toward me; Spider circled out of my range. "Someone made that happen. Who told you?"

I spun, turning so my back was to the squad car, keeping them both where I could see them. "I can't say."

"Who can?" Spider pressed.

"Hailey?" Jeff asked.

"I can't say."

"I can ask her." Jeff smiled.

"Leave her alone." I snarled. "She didn't tell me; no one she talked to recognized Angelo-"

"Who did?" Spider pressed. "I don't see what the issue is? Just tell us who told you."

"Why do you need to know?" I asked warily; I didn't like the undercurrent I felt from them, it was tugging worse than usual. "I can't see how it would matter to you."

Jeff grinned; a sure sign he was losing patience. "This is my job. Catching the bad guy. I need a name, Beth. Who told you?"

You are the bad guy, I wanted to say. I knew better. "He didn't do it."

"*He* might know who did." Jeff said.

I winced, not meaning to give even that much away. At least it would keep Jeff from leaning on Hailey. "Jimmy did it."

"Maestro?" Spider snorted.

"He ordered it." I said. "I heard-"

"You heard what?" Jeff scoffed at that idea. "Family is everything." That definitely was an accusation; my heart constricted, choked by guilt, and by fear. "You think Maestro would take out his own nephew?"

"He must have." I said carefully; Jeff shook his head and took another step closer, not liking my answer. "I saw him last night; I spoke with Jimmy, and I ate at his table."

Jeff froze. "You lying to me?"

"You know I'm not." I said. "I wouldn't lie about something like this."

"But you'd lie about other things?" Jeff asked. His tone had changed, becoming soft, silky smooth: dangerous.

"How did you get close enough to see Jimmy?" Spider over-rode Jeff, focused on the task at hand. I might have thanked him, but I knew he hadn't done it for my benefit. Someone must have been pushing them hard.

That was their problem. "Nigel got us in."

"Essex?" Jeff looked confused. "How does he rank?"

"Nigel's a high value customer; his company brings a lot of business to Grotto, and Jimmy owns Grotto." Jeff and Spider shared a look; that was news to them, and it bothered them. Good. It would get their focus off of me. "Nigel asked to speak to Jimmy, and we were brought straight up-"

"It's Nigel now?" Jeff asked.

My heart pounded. I ignored that, hoping he'd forget I said it. It was a slim hope. "I showed Jimmy my phone. He said he was happy to get Dr. Essex back his car; it embarrassed him that his nephew took it. He said he'd do everything in his power to maintain a good relationship-"

"Hardly a death threat." Spider pointed out.

"Unless that was what he thought the Sept wanted." I said.

"Why would he think that?" Jeff asked; if he were a cat, his ears would have been flat against his skull.

I winced.

"Beth?" Jeff barked.

41

I flinched.

Jeff trudged closer; I backed up till the back of my knees hit the car's bumper. "What did you do?"

"I just wanted his car back–"

"Who told you where he was?"

"It doesn't matter–"

"Assume it does."

"To who?"

"That doesn't matter to you." From someone else I might have laughed at the irony, the almost word for word repetition of my own words back to me; from Jeff, I took it as a threat.

I couldn't tell; I'd promised Evan. "It's way past that." I deflected.

"You're not understanding the situation." Jeff was really getting impatient, bordering on irritated. "It's–"

"There's something worse." I broke in.

"How?" Jeff asked. "What could be worse?" He tilted his head, considering, parsing what I'd said, making connections. "Maestro thinks Essex is Sept." He reasoned it out. "Why does he think Essex is Sept?"

"It was the way Jimmy said what he said, and the way he looked at me."

Jeff tilted his head. "How did he look at you?"

"Like he was afraid of me. Like he thought I was higher up the food chain than he was."

"Maestro's no respecter of women."

"He is if he thinks they're Sept property."

Jeff tensed. "Why would he think that, Beth?"

"Because of the Sigil I was wearing." My voice came out very small. "I put it on at Albro to get through the door but I forgot to take it off–"

42

"You forgot!" Jeff's fist came down on the car beside me, denting the hood; I whimpered. I knew better than to move. "You weren't supposed to have it at all-"

"I know - I didn't even think I still had it." I was pleading, making excuses, and hating myself for it; Jeff winced. "I thought..." His expression clicked, pieces swirled into place. "You put it there-"

"What?" Spider said, looking sharply from me to Jeff.

"-when you broke into my van."

Jeff smiled. "You're still my girl."

"Are you insane!" Spider roared at him. "Do you realize what you've done?"

I used the distraction to sidestep away.

"I know what I've done." Jeff's hand clamped onto my arm before I could get very far. "I made a mistake; I never should have let her go."

"She's gonna get us all killed!" Spider lunged for me; I closed my eyes, bracing for impact.

Jeff blocked him. "She'll fix it."

Spider shoved his chest; Jeff didn't budge an inch. "The only way you fix this mess is to get on your knees and beg, and turn her over to the Tribune-"

"No." Jeff's grip tightened; my adrenaline was so high I could barely feel it.

"They're going to want a head, but they're not getting mine!" Spider snarled. "This will blow back on us! She made this mess-"

"She'll clean it up." Jeff said.

Spider laughed incredulously.

"They want a head," Jeff reasoned, "They'll get Maestro's."

Spider tilted his head. Then he smiled.

43

My heart stopped beating.

"Keep your phone on, baby." Jeff ordered. "When I call, be ready to move."

I couldn't swallow; my heart had moved into my throat. I nodded.

"That's my girl."

7

Involvements

The squad car backed out of the driveway and rolled away. My legs gave out as soon as Jeff's eyes were off me; I crumpled like a marionette with its strings cut, my body shaking and twitching and gasping for air.

"Beth!" Evie came tearing out of the house and tried to pull me up. "What did he do to you?"

I laughed hysterically.

Evie couldn't get me up, so she knelt in the dirt beside me and held me tight. "I'm sorry." She said; I clung to her for dear life. "Marco's still in the hospital; so your dad's on his way, and-"

"No!" I reared back, terror filling me. "NO! He can't-"

"He's here." She said as Dad's van pulled into the drive. She winced. "And so is your mom."

"No." I tried to push up, but my legs were too wobbly to hold me.

The van stopped, and both my parents got out.

Shame and fury filled me; the shame at myself, the fury at myself. I'd made this mess. I needed to clean it up. I took a deep breath in, and forced myself to my feet.

"Beth," Dad didn't even close his door in his rush to get to me. "Did he hurt you?"

I snuggled against his chest, but only for a moment. "He didn't touch me."

"That's not what I asked." Dad said.

"He's not the issue." I backed away from him, and couldn't look him in the eye.

"Then what is?" My mother demanded. Her voice was like a slap; she still took Jeff's side. She still didn't believe he could do any wrong. She still didn't know. I still couldn't tell her. It stung.

"I..." I shook my head, unable to form a thought let alone a sentence to explain any of what had happened, or what I had to do. I didn't know. Yet. I deflected. "Is Hailey at the office?"

"It doesn't matter." Dad said. "Jeff is the issue here-"

"He's really not." I said. "I am. I messed up-"

"You've had another affair?" Mom sideswiped me with that one.

"No, but thanks for going low." I snarled. "It's nice to know what a high opinion you hold of me."

Dad stepped between us, blocking Mom from my view. "What happened?" He barked at Evie, trying to pull this mess away from the fire before it exploded.

"I don't know." She started to cry; Mom turned her back on me and hugged her. "I was asleep and then they were yelling at Beth and-"

"They?" Dad asked. "Spider, too?"

"Valentine was released." I crossed my arms, and said what was safe.

"What?" Mom was furious. "He shot Jeff-"

"And we caught him red handed," I added. "We documented

46

him in the act, and they still let him go."

"Have you spoken to Patience?" Dad asked.

"Not yet." I sighed in relief, clutching at the idea like a drowning man just thrown a life preserver. "That's next on my agenda."

"Then get on it." Dad gave me a task, an order to follow; he knew I needed it. "And keep me apprised. He can't get away with this."

"No." I agreed. "He shouldn't."

"We're on our way to see Marco." Dad said. "If you need-"

"I'll call." I promised. I lied. I couldn't involve him in this. I couldn't risk him. Not again.

Dad hugged me. Mom kissed Evie's forehead, and got into the car. She didn't even look at me. I tried not to care.

"You need to tell her." Evie said.

"I can't." I wrapped my arms tight around my middle.

Evie hugged me, and didn't say what I knew she was thinking. "What's going on? Really?"

"I don't know." I compressed my lips. "I need to find out." I kissed her cheek. "Thank you."

"Be careful." She ordered unhappily.

"I'm trying."

The look she gave me spoke volumes. She went back into her house. I locked myself in my van, pulled out my phone, and tried to figure out a plan.

Jeff hadn't told me much of anything, and I doubted he ever would, and I'd had enough of him for one lifetime anyway. Whatever it was he wanted me to do, I wanted no part of. I had to figure a way out of this mess for myself, and do it before he could reel me in with whatever net he was casting. I had to move fast.

Pope was a long shot - last night was probably a fluke; I wouldn't get something out of him without something in return, and I didn't have anything he wouldn't already know. I needed more info before I went to Patience, a clearer image of what I was looking at. I tried my brother Johnny; no answer. I wondered if that was deliberate. I called Stuart Proust, medical examiner for Metro Police.

"Dover?" Proust answered his phone.

My jaw clenched at hearing my married name, and I made a mental note to call the phone company about my display. Again. "Knox. I need-"

"To stop bothering me. You don't work for the city anymore; I don't have to answer to you anymore." He hung up.

Darn it. I didn't have a choice. I went over his head.

"Dover?" Metro Police Chief Colleen Patience, my former boss, answered.

"Knox."

"You need to change that." Patience said. "One way or another."

I didn't want to touch that. "I'm working on it."

"What are you working on now?"

"Angelo Maes-"

"Not on the phone." She barked. "One hour. You know where?"

"I'll be there, but I need a favor first-"

"You're pushing things, girl."

"Proust's pushing his weight around-"

"Then push back harder." She hung up.

I sighed, and checked the time. 9:10. Nigel! Darn it. I dialed his number.

"You're standing me up." Nigel answered.

48

"I'm so sorry, something unexpected-"

"It must be quite something, or else I've seriously misinterpreted-"

"You haven't." My voice hitched. "If I'd had a choice-"

"We always have a choice, Miss Knox."

Darn it, he was angry, channeling his inner granite. "Except when we don't, and-"

"Must you argue everything?"

"Everything I don't agree with. I can't help it. I'm Irish, and I'm a red-head. Just in case you hadn't noticed."

"I noticed. Were you born in Ireland?"

"Seventh generation Canadian; just don't tell my father."

He laughed. Bitterly. But he laughed. Then he sighed. "Can I at least know the something that's keeping you from me?"

I felt sick inside, knowing I was going to end that laughter. "I take it you haven't heard the news today?"

"What news?"

"Angelo Maestro was found dead this morning. Murdered."

"Oh my word." He exhaled heavily. "Is this on me?"

"No." I said instantly, wanting to protect him. "I don't know." I course corrected, knowing he would prefer the truth, no matter how uncomfortable.

"But you think it likely."

"I'd like to argue that..."

"Can we meet now? I need... I don't know what I need, and I don't like being in this position."

"I know the feeling." I assured him. "It's pretty much the standard in my line of work, but I really don't want to involve you any-"

"Bethany, I'm already involved, and very likely responsible-"

"You had nothing to do with it-"

49

"So you say." He said. "Now. Last night you were quite sure it was my doing-"

"I never should have taken you with me."

"But you did." He reminded me soberly. A little too soberly?

"Guilt trip?" I struggled not to laugh. "Really?"

"They seem to work effectively on you."

"Oh, good grief." I nearly gave in. "No one would blame you-"

"Except possibly the Sept? Or Maestro? Or myself."

"This isn't on you."

"Then let's prove it." He said. "Absolve me. Cleanse my conscience. You've cleared me before-"

"You haven't been accused this time-"

"Bethany. Please? I need to be sure in myself."

I closed my eyes and compressed my lips. "Dead Man's Island in one hour."

"How fitting." Nigel's voice was solid granite, cold and rigid as stone; he was upset. He had a right to be. "I'll bring coffee."

"Bring three." I said. "We're meeting someone."

"Who?"

"A friend." I hoped.

8

A Shocking Development

I slid behind my wheel and drove to the Medical Examiner's office. My white van fit in a little too nicely amidst the refrigerator trucks parked in the lot. It always made me uncomfortable to come here, but I set my teeth, pulled a sweater on over my sun dress, and made myself go inside, determined to get it over with as fast as I could.

I wished I'd worn a parka. It wasn't really cold inside, it just looked that way, everything gleaming chrome and shiny white tile and that antiseptic, beyond-sterile smell to the place that made me shiver.

No one was at the reception desk, so I rang the buzzer and paced the length of the waiting area while I waited for an answer. Stuart Proust himself answered my call, glaring as he pushed through the steel door that separated the front area from his work space.

"You know what your problem is?" He demanded, probably rhetorically.

"I don't take no for an answer?" I smiled sweetly. "I need everything you have on Angelo Maestro. The sooner you help me, the sooner I leave you alone."

"You don't have-"

"I just spoke to Patience and she's not in a good mood." I dropped her name, conveniently leaving out what she'd actually said. "Open the door already."

He threw up his hands and grumbled under his breath, but buzzed me in. "Follow me." He led the way down the hall, second door on the right. "Don't-"

"Touch anything. I know the drill."

Proust grunted, and flicked on the fluorescent overhead lights. "What do you need to know?"

"Everything." I said, looking at the body lying on the slab. It was definitely the kid from last night. He looked so young. It broke my heart. I checked the date of birth on his tag; only 19. "What killed him, when, where was he found? The usual."

"I'm having trouble picking out an exact time of death-"

"Why?"

"Bodies in water..." He sighed in frustration. "It messes up the temperature reading. Then there's the bloating and the-"

I cut him off quickly, not needing that mental image enforced. I'd seen more than my share already. "Drowned, then?"

"Dumped; he was dead before he hit the water, and from the chains wrapped around him, not meant to be found. Best guess puts it sometime after midnight, before 3." He shrugged helplessly.

"I took a picture of him shortly after nine, and Nigel had his car returned before midnight; assuming he was still alive when the car was returned, you're probably correct."

"I usually am." Proust pointed out.

I didn't argue the point. "Where was he found?"

"He was fished out of the harbor - literally, a trawler hauled him in with their catch, just before six this morning."

"Where?"

"Ask your ex."

I raised an eyebrow.

"I don't do salvage," Proust held up his hands defensively. "I just work the body."

"What killed him?"

"Shock, near as I can tell."

"Shock?" I was shocked.

"Shock, and what looks like an underlying heart condition resulting in an aortic tear," He held up the kids heart to show me the damage as if I could recognize what it was as easily as he could, and laughed when I shuddered. "Death probably would have happened soon, but this made it happen a lot sooner." He put the heart back where I thankfully couldn't see it anymore.

"So it wasn't murder, then?" I asked.

"What? No, it was murder. It was just pointless. If the killer'd just waited a few weeks, he would've died anyway."

"The killer probably didn't stop to consider that angle." I rubbed my temple, wondering what angle I needed to take. "He was so young to die of shock."

Proust wrinkled his nose in confusion, not following that line of logic, then he grinned. "Electrical shock."

"Oh, good grief."

He laughed, and pulled down the sheet to show me Angelo's chest. "Looks like someone hit him with battery connectors, here," He pointed out the wounds. "Here, and here."

"Repeatedly." I noted the number of burns. "Poor kid."

"Probably had it coming." Proust shrugged.

"Why?" I asked. "Did you know him?"

Proust lifted Angelo's arm, turning it to show me the tattoo on the inside of his wrist; a red circle, the serpent devouring itself. Sept. "That's all I need to know."

I needed to know a whole lot more. "Thanks, Proust."

I took my leave of him, glad to get outside into fresh air. I looked over at the police station parking lot next door, and saw the squad car with the fresh dent in its hood. Fury drove out caution. I took a gulping breath and walked without letting myself stop to think into the station. The front was insane, as usual. I skipped past the reception desk unnoticed in the chaos, took a left after the meeting rooms, and stopped at the entrance to the bull pen. Patience had her door shut tight, but she wasn't the one I needed to talk to now.

"Hey, it's Scarlet!" Someone shouted.

I winced, hating that Spider's new nickname for me had stuck.

Jeff looked up from his desk in the center of the room, frowning.

"Everything alright?" My brother in law, Ray, asked from his desk at the back of the room.

I nodded my head to Ray, and looked at Jeff. "I need a word."

Jeff followed me down the hall to the first empty meeting room, Spider on his heels.

"What are you doing here?" Jeff asked. "I told you to wait till-"

"Out." I directed Spider.

"Baby-"

"I'll talk with you, but not with him leering at me like that."

"Like what?" Spider snarled at me.

"Beat it." Jeff told him.

Spider swore, but left.

Jeff closed the door, wrapped his arms around me, and lowered his mouth toward mine.

"No!" I back-stepped and raised my arms to block him.

"Baby-"

"I'm not yours anymore!" I twisted out of his grip. "I'm not here for that."

"Then what are you doing here?" Jeff skipped over hurt and went straight to furious. "I told you to wait-"

"You didn't tell me enough." I moved to one of the low chairs, making myself as small and non-threatening as possible, keeping my voice soft, not wanting to add any fuel to the already smoldering fire that was my ex. "I just saw Angelo's body, and the tattoo on his arm; he's Sept?"

Jeff's jaw clenched, refusing to answer. He didn't need to answer. "Who told you who he was?"

"Why does it matter?" I asked, and could tell by his expression I wasn't going to get an answer to that question. I changed the subject. "Was this a Sept hit? It looks like their handiwork-"

"No." Jeff snapped. "I don't know." He corrected himself.

"How can you not know?"

"They don't tell me everything."

"Since when?"

"They're hardly telling me anything." He paced the floor. "I don't know what's going on."

"Who does?"

"No one that will talk to you."

"Will they talk to you?" I asked. "Jeff?"

"They let me get shot, and let Valentine get away with it." He snarled. "What do you think?"

"I think you should have stayed away-"

"Thanks for that." He snorted. "We're done-"

"I'm sorry." I said quickly, darting between him and the door. "I need answers-"

55

"I don't have them." He backed down, pacing deeper into the room, leaning against the far wall, pushing off again, never still for long.

"Where was Angelo found?" I nodded to the wall map, determined to prove he had at least a few answers. "Proust said you knew-"

"Proust's full of himself."

"No argument here."

Jeff grinned. His amused grin. If that had been the only one... "Angelo was found right around here." He thumped his knuckle on a spot near the harbor mouth. "There's a bit of a ledge he must have snagged on, or he'd never have been picked up. The way the currents move, he must have been dropped around here." He circled another spot with his fingertip, east of where Angelo's body was found.

"That's not far from Sculper's Inlet."

"Maestro's grounds; not Sept territory." Jeff pointed out. "Maestro." He emphasized. "Not Sept."

"Maestro doesn't work where he eats," I casually mentioned. "And you'd think he'd show his own nephew more respect... Family is everything."

Jeff glared at the map so hard I was surprised he hadn't burned a hole in it. "I know what you're doing."

"What am I doing?" I asked.

He turned that glare on me. His nostrils flared. His hands balled into fists. "You're trying to manipulate me-"

"I'm trying to understand why Maestro would act so out of character." My heart was pounding so hard they could probably hear it in the bull pen. "He's smart and he's careful; this looks sloppy and obvious. It doesn't make sense."

Jeff turned his glare back to the map, looking for an answer that wasn't there. He tilted his head, his fists turned back into hands. "You think it's a message to Maestro?"

"You tell me?" I asked. "How likely was it that Angelo's body just happened to snag where it would be found? Do you really think that happened by accident?"

Jeff put on his poker face, a sure sign he was considering the idea. Or that he was shutting me out.

"You really think Maestro did it?" I probed carefully.

"You're the one who suggested it." He pointed out.

"I'm not always right."

Jeff grunted agreement.

I compressed my lips. "I don't always have the right information. Why wouldn't you tell me who Angelo was?"

"It's complicated."

"You didn't know." I reasoned - his jaw tightened and his nostrils flared; he was angry - I was right. "But Spider did?"

"Spider knows everyone."

"Why wouldn't he tell me?"

"I don't know."

I looked into his eyes, trying to figure out if he was telling me the truth. It was such a rare occurrence... "Spider's keeping things from you?" My heart lurched, shocked. "Trouble on the home front?"

"Mind your mouth." He shoved me back against the table.

I cut my eyes away, letting him think I'd backed down until he let off. "Was focusing on Jimmy Maestro your idea, or his?"

Jeff looked troubled. "Mine."

I raised an eyebrow.

"Mine." He repeated.

"You're sure Maestro's the right target?"

He frowned at the map. "It'll make the Sept happy."

57

"That's the goal?"

He glared at me.

"You were shot, and they let Valentine walk away." I reminded him. "They've never had your-"

"Mind your mouth." Jeff stepped toward me so he could loom over me, his fingers twitching.

I looked away, nodded; he backed down a second time. I wouldn't get a third. I probed carefully, looking for answers, not looking to push him. Yet. "What's your plan?"

"I'm working on it." He said. "Head home; I'll call-"

"Don't bother." I headed for the door. "I'll make my own plan."

He grabbed my arm. "Where do you think you're going?"

"To find the answers you don't have." I twisted from his grip, knowing how that would goad him. "That's my job." That was really pushing it, but what was luck for if not to be tempted?

I'd probably pay for it later, but I'd have to deal with it then; there wasn't time now. I left the station with shoulders back and head high, and didn't collapse into a gasping, shaking mass until I reached my van. I'd done what I needed to do; I'd planted seeds in Jeff's head. Now all I could do was hope they'd bear fruit.

9

Area of Influence

I pulled into the parking lot first, just as the first fat raindrops began to fall. Choppy, angry little waves were splashing against the rocky banks surrounding the park. No one else was there. Unsurprising, given the weather. And the location. Dead Man's Island came by its name honestly, and most people weren't comfortable with the idea of walking over hundreds of unmarked graves. Given the skeletons I had in my closet, a few hundred more didn't bother me.

I still had half an hour before Patience and Nigel were due. I stepped into the back of my van and converted my bed into table mode. That reminded me I hadn't eaten, and that I had thwarted Nigel's breakfast as well. Well, I wouldn't be a Knox worth the name if I didn't feed my guests. My mother would disown me. She practically already had. I ignored that thought as I opened my fridge, dug out a few mushrooms, a corner of cheddar, and some slightly wilted spinach, chopped and threw it all in a pan with some beaten eggs to make a conciliatory frittata to soothe my conscience, and popped the whole mess into the oven to bake.

The rain had turned into a weak and desultory drizzle, and the oven made the small space feel muggy, so I opened the rear doors to the scent of hemlock and a view of the North West Arm. The view was promptly ignored as I pulled out my notebook and wrote down all I knew about Angelo Maestro and the events of the last dozen or so hours. It was precious little, and I didn't like what I was seeing. It made me angry.

This poor kid had died afraid, and in pain. Someone had been angry with him, and hurt him before he died. Had the killer meant to kill him? Did it matter? The fact was he was dead, and someone had gone to great lengths to cover their tracks. Or had they? Finding Angelo's body in Maestro's territory seemed too convenient, too obvious. Someone had wanted him found. Who? Why? What was the point? I needed a clear motive. I tapped my paper with my pen, trying to find a solution. I had Jimmy Maestro's name on one side, and a whole lot of Sept connections on the other, but nothing like a clear direction to follow. Yet. I needed more information. I hoped Patience had something I could use.

"Knock, knock." Patience poked her head through the sliding door. "Smells good. I'm starving."

"I figured you hadn't eaten."

"Never enough time."

"I remember." I gave her a hand in, and pulled the frittata from the oven just as Nigel's teal sports car pulled up alongside my van. "We have company."

Patience raised an eyebrow but didn't protest. If Nigel's presence had bothered her, she would have. She slid into the banquette and reviewed my notes.

"Morning." Nigel handed me a packet of scones to go with our coffee, and a bouquet of morning glories.

"They're lovely, thank you." I would have kissed his cheek, but given his rigid posture decided not to risk a rebuff.

He looked disappointed, and I felt the weight of another mistake pile on top of the growing heap pressing down on my shoulders.

I waved Nigel in, and he made his way to the bench across from Patience. "Chief Patience?"

"Essex." She didn't look up from my notes, but nodded to Nigel as she took one of the coffees he'd brought.

I divvied up the frittata, heaped the scones on a plate, and slid in beside Nigel.

"You're not a bad little cook." He seemed shocked by my skills; I squeezed his hand.

"You think there's a Valentine connection?" Patience tapped the papers and got to business between bites.

"The Sept tattoo on Angelo's wrist makes one." I said, hoping she'd confirm it, but she said nothing. Darn it.

"Valentine?" Nigel asked.

"The man over your shoulder." I said.

"Ah." He made the connection. "Then I take it this Valentine is Sept, and it seems young Maestro was Sept, and that they were near the same location at the same time last night is likely not coincidence. That's an unexpected development."

"The right hand doesn't always know what the left hand is doing." I agreed. "Or it knows, and chooses not to mention…" I looked at Patience with hopeful anticipation that she would choose to mention exactly what it was that we were dealing with here.

Patience's jaw tightened, but she took another bite of frittata, not contributing anything. Darn it.

"Why would Angelo have joined the Sept?" Nigel wondered.

"Uncle Jimmy wasn't flashy enough for Angelo?" I posited.

"And Uncle Jimmy wasn't pleased by it." Nigel said.

"It could tarnish the family reputation to have his nephew seen working for the competition." I said.

Patience didn't bat an eye, and I took her lack of denial as confirmation I was on the right track. Or the track she wanted me to follow? I leaned back, considering her carefully.

"And I was the one that brought it to his attention." Nigel blew out a breath. "Then his death is my fault–"

"It's not your fault," Patience finally put in. "Not entirely."

"That's not entirely a consolation." Nigel said stiffly.

"And hardly fair." I put in, furious for him.

"Who said life was fair?" Patience huffed at me. "Sometimes life deals you a bad hand–"

"A bad hand?" I asked. "Jeff was shot, Valentine walked, and then this kid turns up dead–"

Patience narrowed her eyes. "I thought you liked Jimmy for it–"

"Someone wants me to like Jimmy for it." I'd hit pay dirt: she winced. "I'm grasping at straws." I said. "I don't have all the information–"

"I can't give it to you." She admitted. "But if there's a way to do it, then you need to give me Maestro."

"Why?" I demanded. "The more I think about this, the more I think Jimmy Maestro wasn't involved."

Patience sipped her coffee, considering her answer. "Sometimes you have to compromise between what's right and what's best–"

"What gives you that right?" Nigel demanded. "Why should you decide–"

"Because the ones that should decide won't." She said. "Drug dealers, rapists, and murderers walk free, while men who make clerical errors on their taxes spend years behind bars. It isn't fair, and it isn't right, and if the elected officials that know better won't choose better, where does that leave me? What choice does it leave me? Not a good one, I'll tell you, but a necessary one. The world will be a better place with men like Maestro off the streets-"

"But if you have to compromise yourself-"

"My boy, we're all compromised. We allow it to go on, we sit back in silence and do nothing while evil men get free reign to do as they will. Allowing that to me is the bigger compromise. It's one I won't make. There isn't enough time-"

"Time for what?" Nigel demanded. "What exactly are we dealing with here?"

Patience chewed her lip and shook her head, shutting down after her outburst. "Angelo's death was not your fault." She was deflecting. "It takes very high-paid people to screw things up this badly."

"How badly?" I stiffened, carefully taking in her reactions; she was tenser than usual, and not nearly as forthcoming as I'd expected. Someone was giving her serious grief over this. It made me nervous. Patience bowed to no one. At least, she never had before. Who could have that kind of power over her? "Who does this effect?"

"Who told you who Angelo was?" Patience countered.

I opened my mouth to tell her, then closed it as her words registered and my stomach tied itself in a tight knot. "Nigel, could you excuse us a moment?"

He looked from me to Patience, reading the tension between us. "Certainly." He bowed himself out, closing the sliding door behind him.

"Sam the second?" She nodded her head to the door Nigel had just closed.

"Nigel the first, and only." I crossed my arms tightly, not comfortable with the comparison she'd just made to my former partner. "They're nothing alike."

"The way you two bounce ideas back and forth..." She contradicted, then she shrugged. "Either way, you make a good team. I'm glad you're not working alone. It's always good to have backup you can trust."

"I wouldn't know." I said caustically.

She raised an eyebrow.

I fixed Patience with a steady gaze, and tried out a sudden theory. "Spider knew who Angelo was, but Jeff didn't. That was your doing. Why?"

Patience settled back uncomfortably, refusing to confirm or deny anything.

Darn it. I pushed. "You cut Jeff out?"

"I thought we could get closer to Valentine without him on this. He's become too volatile without you around to moderate his behavior–"

"I am not responsible for his behavior–"

"Whether you like it or not, the simple fact is you are." She slammed her fork down, furious. "You kept him under control. I didn't think I could trust him not to lash out, and last night he proved my theory was right. We can't afford this loss! Who told you who Angelo was?"

"Who wants to know?"

"That's need to know, and you don't need to–"

"If you want an answer, I need answers–"

"It's beyond my area of influence." She warned me not to pry anymore. "I need to know who told you."

"For who?"

"For me!" She shoved her plate away, leaning across the table so we were eye to eye. "I want to know."

I didn't believe her. "Why?"

"Just tell me!"

"I promised my source I wouldn't give him up, and I won't break my word to him-"

"Him." She huffed, leaning back, tapping her lip. "There's only one person it could be-"

"There's multiple people it could be-"

"Pope." She picked the only one it was.

"No! He's a friend-"

"He's a traitor. He must have warned Valentine we were coming. Valentine knew! The 'trade' you witnessed was a play-act, and it made us look bad-"

"Valentine shot Jeff." I protested.

"And claimed self-defense." She scoffed. "Given Jeff's history with the Sept and Valentine in particular we had no choice but to drop him, so he gets off Scot-free. Again! Valentine always knew too much about our operations - he'd had the drop on our boys. All of that stopped when Pope went away, but it all started again when he got out. We should have had Valentine last night! We would have if not for Pope. He's the link-"

I shook my head, not believing it. "Where's the link between Pope and Angelo?" I wondered. "You're sure it's him?"

"You just confirmed it."

I closed my eyes. I didn't want to see. I didn't want to know. My eyes snapped open. "It could be coincidence-"

"The simplest answer is the right one-"

"The simplest answer is the most convenient. There could be another explanation. You need to take the time-"

"I don't have the time!" She pointed her finger at my throat where the necklace had been. "Your little display last night took any time I might have had and-"

"How?"

"You messed this up-"

"Do not put this on me!"

Patience narrowed her eyes, then whipped out her phone. "Pope." She barked the one word to the person on the end of the line, and hung up.

"Who did you tell?" I demanded.

"It's out of my hands-"

"Who!" I slammed the table.

"Quit trying to-"

"I don't quit." I snarled.

"Except on Jeff, and on your team, and on me!" Her attack was savage; it was meant to be.

"You knew!" I struggled not to cry. "You knew everything Jeff did-"

"You knew the bigger picture!" She accused me. "You were my in!"

"It was too much-"

"And now we're living with the consequences of your weakness."

I looked away.

"This could have been done, and you would have been free to walk away-"

"It was too much."

"We've lost too much-"

I pressed my hands to my abdomen, holding in the agony. "I lost everything-"

"The Sept took my son from me-"

"I didn't even get to have mine!"

Patience looked away that time.

"It was too much." I repeated. "You used me, made me a pawn in your game, one you were willing to sacrifice. It wasn't worth it. You asked too much."

"I had too much faith in you." She stood. "And because of that they've moved beyond my reach. They get away with everything-"

"No!" I protested. "They won't-"

"Getting at the Sept through Angelo was my last shot."

"Angelo?" I demanded, thoroughly confused. "How?"

"Leverage." She snarled.

"Blackmail?" I translated.

"I've had Spider trailing him for weeks; we had enough to hold over his head. He was set to rise in the Sept - we could have turned him! We could have used him to get at Valentine and Maestro both! If you hadn't revealed him to Jimmy and gotten him killed - you've blown this all apart!"

"Angelo was Jimmy Maestro's nephew; he wouldn't have touched him." I shot back desperately. "You haven't played all the angles."

"What angles?"

I didn't have that answer. Yet. And I didn't know how much I could trust her. I didn't know who was controlling her. I deflected. "The serpent always devours itself..." I said. "There's trouble in the ranks, and I may have made things worse. I still have a small area of influence..."

She tilted her head, looking at me from another angle. "What have you done?"

"I ticked off my ex."

Patience smiled.

10

Another Angle

Patience left, and I leapt into action. "Nigel!" I called and he walked around the side of the van. "You were listening?"

"I heard every word." He said. "I assumed that's why you asked me to be here."

I compressed my lips, not sure why I'd asked him. Had I asked him? Did it matter? He'd helped me before, but this wasn't like before.

"Was I wrong?"

I closed my eyes. Patience had been right about one thing; I had no one else I could trust. No one else would trust me. I shook my head. "I can't do this alone."

"How can I help?"

"You can drive." I grabbed my bag and locked the van door.

He held the door for me, then slid behind the wheel of his car. "Where?"

"Grotto."

"You're sure?"

"You have a better suggestion?"

He drove.

I texted Johnny to collect my van, and called Hailey. "I need Pope's number."

"Why would I have it?" She asked.

"Hailey, they're after him."

"Who?"

"Everyone. He needs to go underground, but he needs to speak with me first." I held my breath while she considered.

"I'll be in touch." She hung up.

"How does Pope fit?" Nigel asked as soon as I put the phone down.

"I hope he doesn't." I said.

"You have a past with him?"

"I've known him since kindergarten; he was friends with my brother, dated my sister-"

"I take it their ending was acrimonious?"

"You could say that." I compressed my lips, debating how much to tell him. It wasn't exactly a secret. "Pope got in with a bad crowd and made some catastrophically stupid choices, and took my sister along for the ride. Literally. She was arrested for street racing, while driving a car that he'd stolen. He panicked and blamed her for that part, too."

Nigel winced. "That's not chivalrous."

"Not so much." I agreed. "Hailey was behind the wheel, but she didn't know the car was stolen. Dad and I had to work hard to prove Pope did that alone. They're not exactly on good terms now."

"But you are?" He asked. "That can't have been easy, investigating a friend."

"To clear my sister." I shrugged. "Family is everything."

"And complicated relationships run in the family?"

"We excel at them." I laughed bitterly. "But hopefully we've

69

learned from our mistakes. I hope Pope has. He worked at the Sept car shop-"

"And not the government approved side?"

"Not always." I conceded. "He's done some stupid things, but he's not a bad guy, and he didn't agree with everything the Sept did-"

"But he didn't leave their employ?"

"They're hard to leave." I frowned; that sounded like a flimsy excuse. And I felt like I was making a lot of justifications. "He overheard things, kept tabs on what was going on, and if things started to get too out of hand he'd let us know-"

"By 'us' I assume you mean the police?"

"Through Jeff or Spider." I confirmed.

"And it appears the information flowed both ways-"

"It might appear that way," I interrupted. "But Jeff wouldn't have told him anything important. Jeff wouldn't tell, period. He gets people to trust him, talk to him, but he doesn't give anything away without a good reason. He had a contact inside the Sept he trusted if he needed to feed information, but that was rare, and never anything that would jeopardize an operation like this. Jeff wants Valentine's head; he wants him taken down. He wouldn't have botched this."

"Spider?" Nigel asked.

I chewed on my lip, considering that. "Spider's a lot of things, but he isn't a rat, and he hates Valentine almost as much as Jeff does. It isn't him, and if it's not either one of them, then I can't see how Pope could be the source of the leak. There's got to be someone else, someone we're not seeing."

"And Valentine?" Nigel asked. "I assume he's one of those 'top tier' members of the Sept you mentioned?"

"Your assumption's correct. He's not the top - no one knows

70

for certain who that is, not at our level – but we know Valentine's close."

"And the sigil was his?" Nigel guessed.

"We think so."

"We think so?" Nigel repeated.

"That's what Jeff assumed when he... found it."

Nigel noticed my stumble. "How did Jeff come by the necklace?"

"It might be safer not to ask."

"Safer for him?" Nigel asked. "Is that your concern?"

"Jeff's not the one I'm worried about. He's still too useful to the Sept; he'd only be lightly disciplined for having it," I shook my head. "Or they might have lauded him for it."

"For what?"

"For daring to put himself forth. Only seven sigils were supposed to have been made; it's a direct challenge to the leadership to take one, and a sign of weakness to lose one."

"So this one is missing."

I compressed my lips. "It's supposed to be."

"Supposed to?" Nigel asked. "But isn't? This is a forgery?"

"This one's real." I said. "One of the leaders has a fake. We thought at the time it was Valentine's, but if the wrong man is accused..."

"Complicated." Nigel said. "What can we do?"

"We?"

"I'm here, and I feel responsible for dragging you into this mess–"

"I'm pretty sure I hauled you in."

"Possibly," He grinned. "I'm a good catch."

I blushed.

"Valentine and Jeff, then." He changed direction. "What's

the story there?"

"It's long and convoluted, and it would be breaking a confidence to tell you everything-"

"Bethany, I can't help if I don't know the details, and you're not giving me many to work with."

"I've given my word." I said, hoping to forestall the argument I could see growing on Nigel's face.

"Under oath?"

I gave him a flat look. "I gave my word."

"What can you say? If this goes to trial and you have to tell this story before the judge, would you still keep part back?"

I crossed my arms around my middle, looking out at the boats on the water as we passed, not seeing them. "Yes."

Nigel leaned back, considering me. "You would lie to protect Jeff?"

"I would leave out what wasn't pertinent." I sighed. "Jeff isn't the issue."

He didn't look like he believed me, but he didn't argue the point. "What could you say? What doesn't break your vow to that man?"

I hated having things kept from me, but I couldn't see a way around it. I hated not telling him more. I wanted to trust him. I wanted him to trust me. I bit my lip, and picked a side. "The safest version; Valentine betrayed Jeff and Spider. The group home they grew up in was run by the Sept; it's where they do most of their recruiting. Get them while they're young... They were certainly got. Valentine set up a job, planted evidence from several Sept hits, and sold Jeff and Spider out-"

"Yet they're on the police force now?"

"They were teenagers, and tried as minors; it was struck from their records when they turned eighteen, but they'll never forgive Valentine for it."

"That can't be healthy."

I shrugged. "It's gotten Jeff in trouble more than once. He tried to leave the Sept because of it, and the man he regarded as his father died because of it." I compressed my lips; if Jeff knew I'd told even that much... "The Sept has such a hold on him still."

"Even after their betrayal?"

"They're the closest thing to family Jeff's ever known." I hung my head; I'd tried to be his family. I was never enough. "He blames Valentine for the betrayal; he can't admit the Sept as a whole is in any way culpable. It would destroy his identity to blame them. Not that Valentine's innocent - we suspect he's responsible for a lot of deaths. I could easily see him being responsible for Angelo's." I compressed my lips; I'd told him this much... "He murdered Chief Patience's son."

"For certain?" Nigel was shocked.

"From the lips of a dying man who claimed to have witnessed the deed."

"Jeff's father figure?" Nigel guessed; I nodded. "It's hearsay, then."

I nodded agreement. "It's enough for us, but there isn't enough proof for the court. Not with the lawyers he can afford."

"Justice has a price?"

"Everything has a price, and Valentine can afford to pay. Or more likely to blackmail and threaten..." I made a mental note to poke into that angle more. "Patience can't let it go-"

"Understandably." Nigel said.

"It's eating her alive." I said sadly. "She's determined to get Valentine behind bars any way that she can, and I can't blame her for it. Valentine shouldn't have gotten away with it. Darren

- her son, was a friend. He was a good man. He didn't deserve to die the way he did."

"And your son?" Nigel asked softly.

I compressed my lips. "I was twelve weeks pregnant... I miscarried. Jeff blames Valentine for that." When he's not blaming me. Anyone but himself...

"Valentine hurt you?"

"I hurt myself." I shrugged. "I was investigating Valentine's activities, and not taking care of myself. Living on coffee, not eating, not sleeping. I pushed myself too hard and my body couldn't handle it. I didn't even know I was pregnant until..."

"I'm sorry, Bethany." Nigel said.

"We're here." I deflected.

Nigel didn't push for anymore. I was grateful for that.

There was no valet at this time of day, and no line; the sign on the door said closed for private function. We went inside anyway, stepping into a space that was quiet, tense, and charged with grief and anger.

We had walked into Angelo's wake.

I had my limits, and this was beyond what I was willing to intrude upon. I tugged Nigel's hand, nodding to the door.

"Let's go." I said softly.

"Let's not." Jimmy Maestro stood between us and the door.

I hadn't seen him move. I had seen that expression on him once before, and was doubly sure now that I never wanted to see it again.

He gave me a look of sheer hatred covered with a layer of rage, and I decided I was wrong; this one was worse. "Upstairs."

My heart started to pound.

Nigel took my arm in his and calmly led the way to the same table we'd been at the night before, looking for all the world like this was his decision, and not because Jimmy Maestro and his three bodyguards that could have played on the offensive line for any football team were directing us there. It was the last place in the world I wanted to be.

That feeling intensified when I saw who was sitting at the table: our concierge; Frederic. He looked lost, completely adrift. It hadn't registered the night before, but he looked an awful lot like Jimmy. Frederic's features were subtler, his manners more refined, but with them almost side by side like this the resemblance was uncanny. Brothers? They must be.

I made another connection, and tested my theory: "You're Angelo's father?"

The look Frederic turned on me was identical to the one Jimmy wore.

Nigel drew in a sharp breath. "We are so sorry for your loss." He told Frederic, and included Jimmy. "If there's anything I can do-"

"You?" Jimmy spat the word.

"I wished the boy no ill, and no harm." Nigel insisted. "And I hope the incidents of last night-"

"What is he talking about?" Frederic demanded, looking at Jimmy.

Jimmy tugged at his collar. Nervous? "You have explaining to do." He barked at Nigel. That sounded a lot like a deflection.

"We have questions." I spoke up.

"You have questions?" Jimmy was incredulous. "You come in here after-"

"After what?" Frederic asked. "What questions? What do you know about my boy?"

"Not enough." I slid into the chair across from him, deciding he was the one most likely to cooperate. "I'm trying to find out who killed Angelo, and why-"

"Why?" Jimmy snarled. "You killed him." He jabbed a finger at Nigel.

"What!" Nigel was irate. "Why would I? My car was returned to me; that was my only concern. My car was returned, we shook on the matter, we made our peace; I had no issue after that-"

"What car?" Frederic looked confused, and then he looked angry; he slammed his fists on the table. "What is going on?"

"A picture's worth a thousand words..." I showed him my phone; Frederic's brows furrowed deeply as he took in his son's image. "Angelo stole Nigel's car last night. That's what brought us here; we were looking for him. Jimmy had the car recovered," Jimmy winced; I guessed he hadn't told his brother any of this. Why? To protect Angelo, or to protect himself? "And we thought the matter settled, until the police told me this morning of Angelo's death-"

"Why would they tell you?" Frederic furrowed his eyebrows, squinting at me.

"Because I'm a private investigator, and they knew I'd been asking about him last night-"

"Investigator?" Jimmy broke in. "You're Sept-"

"No woman is Sept." I repeated by rote.

Jimmy sat down hard. "You're not Sept?" He looked at Nigel. "Then you're not Sept either?"

"No man is Sept." Nigel quipped. "Not that I've seen."

I could have smacked him for sounding so flippant. "Nigel is most assuredly not Sept, and I owe them no loyalty."

"What does the Sept have to do with my son?" Frederic asked.

"Angelo had a Sept tattoo on his wrist." I said; Frederic closed his eyes. "A red circle - a snake eating its own tail."

He nodded his head. "I didn't know what it was; Angelo didn't tell me."

I watched Jimmy's reaction carefully. He knew. Why hadn't he told his brother? Did I play that card, let Frederic know? What else was Jimmy hiding? I stayed mum, hoping I was making the right call. "The car Angelo took last night - Nigel's car, was parked outside a police take-down of one of the Sept leaders." Jimmy tugged his collar again. Why? Maybe it was too tight? "I think there may be a connection-"

"Did the Sept kill my boy?" Frederic's voice broke as he asked.

"I don't know." I answered honestly. "But I'm trying to find out."

"Why?" He narrowed his eyes at me. "Why do you care-"

"Because he was just a kid, and he didn't deserve to die." Frederic wasn't buying it; I told him the truth. "And I lost my son because of them." I tried and failed to blink back tears, furious with myself; Frederic leaned back, examining me closely, and nodded his head, deciding my concern was genuine. Sometimes being a sucker pays off. "The Sept has brought nothing but grief into my life." Nigel squeezed my fingers under the table; I squeezed back, grateful for his presence. "Any way that I can thwart them, I will."

"Thwart's a good word." Frederic smiled that same terrible smile his brother used. It was kind of growing on me, at least from him. The vibes from his brother were making me nervous.

Jimmy seemed agitated and defensive. The effects of grief, or something more? I couldn't tell, and I didn't have enough rapport built up to press him. The way he was glaring at me, I doubted I ever would.

I focused on Frederic. "I don't know for sure if the Sept killed Angelo or not, but if they did, and I can prove it..."

Nigel looked Frederic in the eye. "We want to see justice

done."

"We want the truth." I insisted. "Did Angelo have any friends, someone that might know about his involvement in the Sept?"

"His cousin." Frederic said. "On my wife's side. Angelo idolized him, he bragged to him; he was always trying to get his approval, trying to impress him. He had the same tattoo - a red circle. I thought that was why he got it done, to be like him."

"His name?" I asked, but I had a strong suspicion about what name he was going to say.

"Evan Pope." Frederic said the name I expected, the grief raw in his voice. "You'll find who killed my boy." It wasn't a request. "You'll get me justice."

"We will." Nigel promised.

I hoped we could keep it.

11

Hide and Seek

"We're sure Jimmy's innocent of Angelo's murder?" Nigel asked as soon as we got outside.

"We're not sure." I waited for him to open the car door for me. "But we're not making an accusation unless and until we are."

"I appreciate that." Nigel gave me a searching look before starting his car. "You're glaring at me."

"I'm not."

"You are." He grinned wryly. "When and how did I put my foot in my mouth?"

I compressed my lips, and quoted him to himself. "No man is Sept."

"You disagree with my estimation?"

"Angelo was Sept." I reminded him. "Frederic might have known, and even been proud of him for it-"

Nigel huffed. "I can't see how-"

"You're projecting your own logic and reasoning onto others; you can't do that in an investigation like this-"

"Why not?" He started the car; it felt dismissive.

"Because it risks putting a potential suspect's back up when we need to be building rapport! We're dealing with heightened emotional responses and potentially any number of neuroses or even psychosis, and we can't afford for anyone to shut us out. We have to go in with the intention to learn what happened, and learn how they think, not push what we think. A murderer is not normal; normal logic and reasoning does not apply. Not that yours is normal–"

"Ach!" Nigel was offended. "You find me abnormal then?"

"Yes." I said honestly. "You're a step above."

I looked away, my face flaming as red as my hair. That was a bit more honest than I'd meant to be. My admission confounded him into silence.

For a few moments. "What's next?" Nigel asked as he drove up the road to his building.

"I have to find Pope," I told him. "Or at least speak to him. That's priority one."

"She persists."

"Relentlessly." I said. "She doesn't have a choice. She won't give herself one."

"Is that your van?" Nigel pulled into his parking lot and parked alongside what was indeed my van, parked directly in front of the front entrance where it couldn't possibly be missed.

"I texted Johnny to move it for me." I frowned at my brother. Johnny was leaning against my van door and did not look pleased with me, as evidenced by the expression he wore, one inherited from our mother. I suppose since he had her dark hair and eyes as well he came by the inheritance honestly, but I didn't find it reassuring. "I knew you had your meeting–"

"Johnny?" Nigel asked coolly. "He's another old friend?"

"You could say that." I sighed. "He's someone I can't do without." I opened my own door.

Johnny crossed his arms. "I have a life, you know."

"Mine might be cut short."

He laughed, but then he saw I was serious. "What's wrong?"

I flared my eyes, not wanting to get into it in front of Nigel. "Johnny, this is–"

Johnny held out his hand, not waiting for my introduction. "You must be Nigel."

"You must be Johnny." Nigel extended his hand in return.

Their expressions changed as their grips tightened, taking the measure of each other. I rubbed my temple, waiting for the testosterone to ebb. Nigel flinched ever so slightly; Johnny smiled, taking that as a win. Oh, good grief.

"Three hours, Miss Knox." Nigel bowed his head to me, his voice as hard as granite, embarrassed that he'd lost.

"Dr. Essex." I returned.

Johnny and Nigel glared at each other before Nigel turned abruptly and went inside. Roosters.

"What's wrong?" Johnny asked again as soon as Nigel was out of earshot.

"What isn't?" I blew out a breath. "We need to find Pope."

"Hailey told me you were looking for him." Johnny said. "He's ditched his phone and gone into hiding; she can't reach him."

"We need to reach him, and we need to do it before anyone else does."

"Who else?"

"Sept." I frowned. "I think." Who had Patience called? Why wouldn't she tell me? I considered calling her, then remembered how quickly she'd gotten me off the phone the last time. Was her line bugged? That might explain a few things, but only a few. There was too much I didn't know. Too much being kept from me. It rankled.

81

"Get in." Johnny nodded to the van with his head, heading for the driver's side. "I know a few places he might be."

"Give me the keys-"

"No way am I getting in a car with you behind the wheel! I have too much to live for-"

"I'm a good driver!"

"I'm better." He smirked at me.

I rolled my eyes, but didn't waste any more time arguing. "Quick stop first," I frowned at my van. "We need a faster car."

"No," He countered. "We need a boat."

Johnny drove my van to the Cormorant Cove Marina. "Is this thing always this slow?"

"You're the one that picked out this model." I reminded him.

"You're the one that insisted on stealth over speed." He retorted.

"Where do we find Pope?" I changed the subject. "And how do you know where he is?"

"He has an aunt out past Sculper's Inlet." He said. "And I know cause I pay attention."

"Who else knows?"

Johnny pursed his lips, exactly the way Dad did when he was considering how best to deliver bad news.

"Johnny?"

"Spider might."

I compressed my lips. "Go faster."

Johnny pushed his foot down on the gas pedal; my van made a rather horrid grinding, squelching sound, and chugged along at exactly the same speed as before.

"This is embarrassing." Johnny shook his head.

I rubbed my temple and laughed. It was either that or cry.

We pulled into the marina, locked up my van, and sprinted

for the dock. Johnny loosed the lines while I pulled off the tarp covering the Hard Knox, and after only three attempts to start the ancient speedboat's engine we were off. Johnny idled us through the busy laneway and out into the Arm, then picked up speed. We skipped over the waves and into the wider harbor, a jet of water pluming out behind us. This thing was old, but she wasn't slow. The wind was cold, the spray it whipped up colder, but at least it wasn't raining too hard. I bundled my hair into a loose braid to keep it out of my face, wishing I'd thought to change into something warmer than my sun-dress and sandals, and tried to bring some of the loose bits of information circling in my head into some kind of order. I still had more questions than answers, too many gaps with nothing to fill them. I hoped Pope could fill them.

"Did you know Pope was related to Maestro?" I asked Johnny.

His lifted eyebrows assured me he didn't. "Who told you that?"

I shot him a sharp glance. That question... I shook my head free of suspicion. Johnny was one of the few persons I could trust to be without ulterior motives. "Maestro himself." I said. "Frederic Maestro." I clarified.

"Frederic?" Johnny wrinkled his nose.

"Jimmy's brother, and Angelo's father. Pope is his nephew."

Johnny pursed his lips as he turned this over in his head. "Pope never mentioned. But it wouldn't be like him to tell - too much like bragging. It's not his style."

"The style of Angelo's murder looks an awful lot like Sept handiwork."

"But you're not buying it?"

"I don't know." I admitted. "I'm second guessing every-thing."

"Over-thinking." Johnny said; he sounded like Dad. "That's always been your problem." Until he sounded like Mom.

I bit my lip to keep in the retort I wanted to make, but I couldn't stop the glare I sent at my brother.

Johnny grinned at me, knowing he'd pushed my buttons, and pushed the throttle. The wind cut through my dress, making me shiver. We hugged tight to the coast line, and I hugged my arms tight to my body to keep in what little warmth I had. We passed the Hardy Point lighthouse and Sculper's Inlet, and turned into a cove so small it wasn't even named on the map. I held the map up, looking closely; this spot was very near where Angelo's body was found. The thought unsettled me. I don't believe in coincidence. What were we going to find here? I really hoped it was answers.

Johnny took us farther into the cove. There were a few houses huddled around a single wharf, their tiny gardens protected from the wind by a row of scraggly trees.

"Which one?" I asked.

"Red shutters." Johnny pointed with his chin. "Want me to come?"

He didn't sound eager. I raised an eyebrow.

"His aunt doesn't like me much."

"Do I want to know why?"

"Probably not." He grinned. "You might not want to mention we're related."

"I'll keep that in mind."

I stepped from the boat and climbed the ladder to the wharf, then continued on to the house with the red shutters bordering the windows. The red didn't end there; it seemed to be a theme. I pushed open the red garden gate and walked the path bordered with a tangle of red roses, red geraniums, and red and white striped petunias. The thick lace curtains in the window twitched; whoever was inside knew I was coming. The door opened before I could mount the steps, and a tiny garden gnome of a woman - dressed in red, of course - with a formidable looking rolling pin in her hands stepped out to bar the way. She looked like a sweet grandmother from a nursery rhyme with her rosy cheeks and frilly apron, but her manner was slightly irritated, and more than a little acerbic.

"Afternoon," I greeted her. "I was looking for Evan-"

"He isn't in my house." She assured me.

"I really need to find him."

"What's he gone and done now?" She demanded. "That boy gets himself in more trouble-"

"As far as I know he hasn't done anything, but trouble's coming anyway. I need to find him before it does."

She squinted at me. "Have you been here before? I'm sure I recognize that red hair-"

"Not me." I held up one of my locks. "Possibly my sister-"

"No." She sniffed in disbelief and tapped her lip, trying to place me. "I know your face from somewhere. I'm sure of it."

"Do you know where I can find Evan?" I asked, redirecting her focus. "Please, it's important I speak with him."

"That's just what that policeman said earlier."

"Policeman?" My heart thudded. "Tall, thin build-"

"He was tall, but he wasn't thin. Not fat mind you; all over with muscles, and I thought I glimpsed a tattoo." She gave a breathless little sigh at his memory.

Jeff, not Spider. Darn it.

"The thin one stayed in the boat."

Oh good grief. "Did you tell them where Evan was?"

"I may have sent them seeking after him in the Narrows."

85

I tilted my head. "But that's not where he is?"

"No, dear." She smiled for the first time. "He's right behind you."

12

Scapegoat

I whipped around so fast I nearly fell over.

"Red." Pope stood on the garden path behind me, arms crossed, not nearly so pleased to see me as he had been the last time.

"You shouldn't be out front." The gnome scolded him, looking meaningfully at the house next door. "If Prunie sees you..." She tsked and shook her head, letting our imaginations fill in the blank about Prunie's nefarious intentions.

From where I stood, it seemed that house had a clear view to the harbor; I wondered if Prunie had seen anything to do with Angelo? I decided that would be my next stop after this visit.

"How did you find me?" Pope didn't seem too concerned about Prunie.

"Johnny." I nodded to the Hard Knox idling out in the cove.

Pope turned and waved him in. "Inside." He directed me.

It was blissfully warm inside the house, and smelled of cinnamon and sugar. It made me think of Hansel and Gretel coming across the witch's candy house in the woods. I wanted to laugh at myself for having such a silly notion, but I felt too uneasy. I told myself it was just my over-active imagination, and tried my best to tamp down the fear growing in my gut.

The red color scheme continued inside, but with hearts added to the theme, from the red heart shaped floor mat at the front entry, to the red heart-covered wallpaper in the kitchen, to the thick lace curtains I could now see were patterns of repeating hearts. The house was clean, but felt cluttered with piles of newspapers and magazines stacked along the walls, and too much furniture - too much for one woman alone. She didn't have a wedding ring on, but she was up to her elbows in dough; maybe she'd removed it while she did her baking? I didn't see any photos of family, but her manner toward me was still chilly so I didn't want to pry into her background. Yet.

Pope tossed me a towel for my wet hair, and directed me to the kitchen table. The gnome put the kettle on to boil and hovered nearby, obviously meaning to include herself in any conversation happening under her roof. Johnny entered the house, looking more nervous than I'd ever seen him. The gnome took one look at him, and picked up her rolling pin.

Johnny winced, and rubbed his neck sheepishly. "Sorry about your teapot."

"That was my mother's teapot." The gnome pointed him to a seat and turned the rolling pin loose on the cookie dough she must have been preparing when I came to the door, sniffing in disgust, and keeping a close eye on Johnny in case he had any more designs on her fine china.

Pope chuckled at them. "Tell me a story, Red."

"I was hoping you could tell me one." I said. "One involving Angelo Maestro-"

"That boy." The gnome interjected, shaking her head. She sounded more annoyed than upset, and that set my teeth on edge. "If he'd only listened..." She tsked.

"Listened to what?" I wondered; she didn't answer.

Pope gritted his teeth, his leg bounced up and down nervously. "I didn't think he'd really do it."

"Who?" I asked.

"Who do you think?" He snapped. He seemed annoyed with me too, but why I didn't know. "What's the deal, Red?"

He wasn't dealing straight; he seemed tense and out of sorts, even more than I'd expected. Maybe I'd expected too much? I switched my line of questions. "The cops think-"

"The cops?" He said scornfully. "They're Sept lackeys - and you led them right to me!"

"They already knew." Johnny informed him. "Remember, Spider was with us when we..." He cleared his throat meaning-fully.

Pope grinned at whatever it was they'd been up to.

"Oh, you boys." The gnome tittered behind her hand.

I didn't want to know. Not that. "Why would the Sept be upset with you?" I asked. "The cops are the ones that think you betrayed them-"

"About what?" Pope asked incredulously.

"Valentine." I said. "Someone must have warned him-"

The gnome gave an indignant squeak and wielded her rolling pin with far more force than necessary.

Pope's eyebrows climbed so high they nearly merged with his hairline. He shook his head vehemently. "I didn't. I'm not a rat-"

"I believe you." I insisted. "How can I convince them?"

"Sounds like they've already made up their minds; I'm the expendable one-"

"Never." The gnome contradicted him.

Pope shook his head. "They're going to expend me."

"You're a convenient scapegoat." I agreed with that much. "But the why of it? Someone is extremely concerned that I found out who Angelo was, and they were desperate to know who told me-"

"They don't know?" Pope sat up hopefully.

"They do now." I said; he slumped in his chair. "Patience guessed it was you, and since Spider and Jeff were here earlier, I'm guessing she passed it on."

Pope's leg vibrated. "You and your big mouth."

The gnome sniffed disgustedly at me, adding an annoyed glare for good measure.

I compressed my lips. "Why was it a secret? They were more concerned about who told me about Angelo then about who might have tipped off Valentine. Angelo had to have been known around Metro-"

"He wasn't, though." Pope said. "He grew up in a small community outside the city, went to a small school where no one knew anything about the Maestro's or the Sept unless something big made it onto the news, and even then no one seriously made the connection to him-"

"He ought to have stayed there." The gnome interjected.

Pope ignored her. "No one in the Sept knew he was connected. He used his mom's maiden name. He was doing his best to hide who his family was."

I wondered how Patience knew? My best guess: Spider. It was his favorite extra-curricular; finding people's deepest secret, and using it against them. Why hadn't he told Jeff? "Just like you were?" I asked. "You never mentioned you were related to the Maestro's-"

"Only by marriage!" The gnome interrupted peevishly. "If

my sister had listened to me, none of this would be an issue."

"None of what?" I asked; she ignored me again, focusing on her cookies instead.

Pope grunted. "How did you find out?"

"Frederic Maestro told me."

All the color drained from his face.

The gnome nearly dropped her rolling pin.

"He said Angelo idolized you, and got the Sept tattoo to be like you; he didn't recognize the sigil for what it was-"

"Like hell he didn't-"

"Evan!" The gnome threatened him with a wooden spoon. "You mind your language!"

"Sorry, Aunt Edna." He said by rote; she nodded, pacified. "Uncle Frederic absolutely knows what the sigil is; he hated that I was Sept, and he wanted Angelo to have nothing to do with them. He wanted me out, and he blamed me for bringing Angelo in."

"Did you?"

"What? No." Pope shook his head vehemently. "I warned Angelo off, but the second he was old enough to live on his own he moved to the city, and he joined up anyway when I was in jail and couldn't talk him down from the idea; the stupid kid always thought the Sept was cool."

"Until the Sept killed him." Johnny shook his head.

Edna banged her rolling pin; Pope looked away.

"Didn't they?" I couldn't figure out their reactions. "What am I missing?" Had I been right in the first place? "You think Jimmy-"

"No, no - not Jimmy." Edna said irritably. "Frederic."

Pope swallowed hard, then reluctantly nodded agreement.

"Frederic killed Angelo?" I rubbed my temple. That had come

91

out of left field. My brain was trying hard to wrap itself around the idea, and struggling to line it up with the facts as I thought I knew them. I was having a hard time with it. Stranger things had happened - children had been murdered by their parents before, but it wasn't something that had even occurred to me when I'd sat across from Frederic earlier that day. Why hadn't it? What had I missed? He'd been so upset. And I'd believed him. Was I slipping? Or projecting? He'd lost his only son, and I'd just had a reminder of losing mine...

"Angelo's father killed him?" Johnny was incredulous; I felt somewhat reassured.

"Maestro and Sept don't mix." Edna clucked her tongue, picked a ring up off the back of the sink and slipped it on her finger, and brought warm cookies fresh from the oven to the table. "Never have, never will." She said pointedly to her nephew.

He crossed his arms across his chest and didn't argue. His leg was thumping like a rabbit's. Why?

"Frederic hates the Sept that much?" I asked, still struggling to believe.

"He told me he'd rather die than see his son join the Sept; he'd rather not have a son at all if that happened." Edna insisted calmly as she poured us each a mug of tea. "If that's not a declaration of intent, I don't know what is."

"You're on good terms with him?" I sipped the hot tea gratefully, finally beginning to warm up. Physically, at least. Edna was giving me chills. I couldn't figure her out, and I didn't like the way Pope was acting. His nervousness was increasing. Why? What was I missing?

"He's my brother-in-law." She nodded. "We have family dinner every Sunday, and we share a box at the Trident once a month. We talk." She wiped a spot off the table with her apron, then put her hand on Johnny's shoulder as she leaned over him to peer at something through the window. "Those police officers are back."

I jumped up to look for myself, but Edna stood in front of me and I could barely make out their shapes tying up at the wharf through the thick lace. "Jeff's persistent."

"They've seen the Hard Knox." Johnny joined us, rubbing at his shoulder. "They know we're here."

"They don't know Evan is." I said. "They don't have to know."

"I'm sick of hiding." Pope said.

"It's only been, what, six hours?" I asked.

"Do you think they'll ever stop looking?" He gave me a flat look. "Do you think that Frederic will let them stop? He convinced himself he had to kill his only son, and he blames me for having to do it! He'll kill me-"

"Not you, dear." Edna said reassuringly. "There's someone he'll blame more."

I tilted my head, trying to make sense of Pope's words. "Frederic will let them? Frederic?"

Johnny blinked incoherently, a confused look on his face.

Pope swore.

Edna swatted his arm with the wooden spoon, but spoke to me. "Jimmy's only the front man. It's Frederic that conducts everything from behind the scenes."

"Including the police?" I asked, the pieces coming together.

"Of course, dear." She patted my hand as if I were a particularly dense child; I felt a sharp prick and wrenched my hand away. A tiny bead of blood welled up on my skin. "He controls the police..."

I closed my eyes as the room began to swim around me. The

93

pieces swirled apart and rearranged themselves again. Edna's words registered; someone he'll blame more: me?

Johnny collapsed on the floor.

My head felt heavy. I could hardly keep my neck up. I made my eyes open. Made them look at her. Hearts swirled through my vision.

Edna twisted the silver ring on her finger and removed it, careful not to let the tiny barb that she'd poked us with poke her. Not barb. Fang. The ring was a serpent, eating its own tail. "And the Sept."

13

Matters of the Heart

I swam through a haze of yelling to consciousness. I struggled to open my eyes. Bits of red floated past. Hearts... Valentines?

"Well how was I to know?" Edna demanded. "You said it was her and her boyfriend that went to Grotto, I just assumed he was the one-"

"He's not her boyfriend." Jeff snarled. "He's her brother."

"Who was with her at Grotto, then?" Edna snapped.

"Nigel Essex." Spider said; I could hear the smirk in his voice. "He's her boyfriend."

I heard a gunshot, and flinched. I blinked. Not a gunshot. A loud bang. I heard it again, my eyes flickered open long enough to see the source of the sound: Jeff smacking the wooden rolling pin against counter top.

"He's not her boyfriend." Jeff emphasized each word with a smack of the pin.

Spider held up his hands in surrender.

My eyes closed and fluttered open; my head lifted an inch before thudding back to the linoleum floor.

"There, you see? I told you she'd wake up." Edna rattled her teacup pointedly, trying to get Jeff's attention.

I could have told her that was a waste of time, but that would require energy I didn't have.

"Baby," Jeff ignored Edna's whiny voice and set the rolling pin down on the counter. "You OK?"

I tried to look around again. "Johnny?"

My brother groaned in response from somewhere behind me. "What hit me?"

"Sept Venom." Jeff told him as he hauled me to my feet. "Just enough to knock you out, and keep you helpless." He smiled as he traced a finger over my cheek, and I couldn't pull away.

My legs wouldn't hold me, so Jeff propped me in a nearby rocking chair. I could see better from this vantage, but it took effort to keep myself from sliding onto the floor.

"Venom, eh?" Johnny managed to push himself to sitting, leaning against the wall, the gaze he turned on Edna full of venom, the one he set on Pope not much friendlier.

The rolling pin rolled off the counter and landed on the floor with a bang, making us all jump. Jeff whirled and whipped his gun out in one fluid motion, trained on the pin. Spider laughed at him. Jeff gave him the finger, and holstered his gun.

"Essex?" Edna tapped her lip, then held her finger in the air as recognition dawned. She bobbed across the kitchen to a stack of newspapers, rifling through the pile till she found the one she wanted: the copy of the Globe with Nigel and I in the heart shaped photo on the cover, dancing together at the Spring Gala. "Oh, I'd say he's her boyfriend. I knew I recognized her! I remembered the heart." She smiled wickedly at me, clapping her hands gleefully. "And his box is across from mine at the Trident. Oh, yes, this will work beautifully."

Jeff snatched the page from her, holding it so tight in his fists the paper crinkled and tore. "You were with him."

My heart stopped beating. My tongue felt like cotton, but I made the words come out. "I was with Victor! I only danced with Nigel to get close to a mark-"

"The picture makes it quite clear." Edna contradicted.

"Nigel's dating Celia Vanderly," I flung out desperately. "Why would he want me?"

Jeff relaxed. Slightly. I inhaled shakily, relieved. He believed me. Nigel would be safe from him.

"Either way." Edna sniffed. "He was with her at Grotto; Frederic believes they are together; that will be enough."

"Enough for what?" I demanded with as much force as I could manage.

"Satisfaction? Vengeance?" She shrugged. "Take your pick. It will shift Frederic's focus from Evan; it's for a good cause-"

"Is that how you justified murdering Angelo?" I spat at her. "A good cause?"

"I didn't kill my own nephew!" She laughed shrilly; I didn't believe her.

"You had a hand in it." I countered. "Did you?" I asked Pope.

"What? No!" He turned white as a sheet, and turned to his aunt. "You said it was Frederic-"

"It was what Frederic wanted." She gave a dismissive wave.

Pope slumped into the nearest chair, stunned, goggling at her; Edna didn't notice his reaction.

Jeff missed nothing. But what would he do about it?

"Not wanting his son to join the Sept and wanting him dead are two very different things." I argued.

"They are the same." She insisted.

"Exactly the same." Jeff agreed with her. "Some people over-think everything." He looked pointedly at me.

97

"Exactly!" Edna patted his bicep.

Jeff took her fingers in his. "But it would probably be best if Frederic didn't know you were involved in his son's death."

"You're so thoughtful." Edna blushed.

"Or your son," I tried out my theory. "Mrs. Valentine."

Edna yelped as Jeff's fingers constricted. Spider winced. Pope swallowed convulsively. No one contradicted me.

"Oh, I'm sorry." Jeff turned on his puppy-dog eyes. "Did I hurt you?"

"My, you are a strong one." Her laughter was a little strained as she shook out her fingers. "But for now, I want him." She took the picture out of Jeff's hand, frowning at Nigel's torn and wrinkled image. "Look how you've mussed it!" She swatted Jeff playfully.

"What do you want done with him?" Spider pointed a thumb at Johnny.

"I don't like complications." Edna frowned. "Kill him." She ordered his death with as much inflection as someone choosing between tea or coffee.

Spider grabbed Johnny by the hair, and flipped out his knife.

"No!" I screamed, and tipped onto the floor trying to get to my brother.

"No!" Jeff barked at the same time; he yanked me up and back into the rocking chair, and clamped his hand over my mouth. "You'll get blood all over Edna's kitchen! Take him out back."

Spider shrugged and put his knife away, then bent to pick up Johnny.

Edna opened her mouth to protest.

"Prunie will see." Pope put in before she could speak - picking up on their game before I did. "Nosy old biddy's always watching out the window."

"Then we'll have to get rid of her, too." Spider grinned; Edna didn't seem upset by this suggestion.

"Sloppy." Jeff tsked. "Two bodies, and then add a missing person in the same area?" He shook his head. "The cops will swarm the place."

Edna shook her head, aghast at the thought. She darted in with her ring and gave Johnny and I another prick each, moving so quickly no one could protest until it was too late. "There, that should do it. No fuss, no mess. Their hearts will stop in a matter of hours, and the cops won't be the wiser." She took in Jeff's uniform. "The real cops." She smiled.

Jeff went rigid, his jaw clenched tight; this wasn't part of his plan.

Any color left in Pope's face drained away. He looked at Edna like he'd never seen her before, and never wanted to see her again.

"Well that takes away all the fun." Spider said.

Edna smiled at Jeff. "But you are right, disposing of more bodies so near the house..." She clucked her tongue. "It just won't do."

I slumped in the chair, consciousness slipping away, and Jeff removed his hand from my mouth. There was no point covering it anymore.

Jeff looked to Spider, and pointed to Johnny. "Take his boat, dump him at the place I tossed Jake's gun."

Spider nodded. "No one would ever find him there."

"They wouldn't think to look." Jeff agreed. "You better give him a hand." He told Pope.

Edna clapped, obviously delighted by the suggestion.

Spider hauled Johnny up and Pope took his other arm to propel him towards the door.

Johnny looked at me, wide eyed. "Beth–"

"Don't worry." Jeff smiled wickedly at my brother. "I'll take care of her."

I bit my lips and hung my head, and couldn't bear to let myself look at Johnny. This was my fault. Hearts began to swirl in front of my eyes.

"And Essex, too." Jeff added softly, so only I could hear.

It was all my fault.

14

Impact

I felt a sharp jab in my arm and came to in Jeff's boat, and wished I hadn't. It was dark. It felt like I was falling. I was freezing cold, even weaker than before, and every joint in my body burned with pain.

"There now." Edna's face resolved into focus and she smiled down at me, a needle in her hand. "That did the trick."

"For how long?" Jeff asked her. He didn't even look at me. It felt like we were married again. On a good day.

"An extra hour or so?" She didn't sound certain. "Long enough for our needs. Long enough for Essex to see her, but be helpless to help her. Frederic is such a romantic; he'll appreciate their tragedy." She gave a breathless little sigh, anticipating the drama.

If my legs had been cooperating, I would have kicked her overboard. As it was, all I could manage was a very forceful glare. Edna didn't seem perturbed. She didn't even notice. Darn it.

I tilted my head, and the falling sensation turned into flying. The sky was dropping down, getting closer, trying to crush me.

I almost threw up. We were in the canal lock, rising up toward the top. The light turned green. Jeff dropped the guide rope he'd been holding, returned to the helm, and piloted out onto Newell Lake.

I tried to roll over and couldn't manage it. I felt like a turtle stuck on its back, all my soft spots exposed. I struggled until I flopped over onto my side. Jeff laughed at me. A burst of fury gave me strength. I twisted onto my front, then pushed up to sitting, trying to blink away the grogginess and the strange gritty feeling in my eyes. My mouth tasted like metal, but not garlic. Not arsenic. I laughed at that.

Jeff looked at me sharply.

Needles are sharp, and fangs are sharp, and cheddar cheese is sharp. I like cheese.

"What's wrong with her?" Jeff snarled.

"She's delirious." Edna shrugged.

Was I talking out loud?

"Yes, Beth." Jeff snapped at me. He was angry. He snaps when he's angry. He's angry when he's afraid. "You're talking out loud."

"Oh." I said, and knew I said it.

I shook my head, trying to clear it, trying to remember if I said anything I shouldn't have.

"Like what?" Jeff asked. "You're still talking out loud."

"Oh." I put my hands over my ears so I wouldn't say anything else.

"Give her the rest." Jeff ordered.

Edna shook her head. "But–"

"We can't take her in like this." Jeff said. "They'll stop her at the doors, and then your plan won't work at all."

Edna huffed. "Oh, very well." She filled the needle and

stogged it into my arm again.

Cold flooded me; it burned its way up my arm and rushed all through me. I whimpered and nearly wept from the pain. I wouldn't give Jeff the pleasure of seeing that. My eyes still felt gritty, but the fog in my head burned away. I shivered and pulled my knees to my chest, wrapping my arms around them, making myself small. "Where are you taking me?"

Jeff grunted. "You'll see."

"What's the plan?"

He didn't bother to answer me.

"We're here." Edna crooned.

I blinked up at the building we were approaching: the Trident Center. It was shaped like a trident. There was a casino and bar on one end, a fancy restaurant and ballroom on the other, and the Crown Auditorium in the middle where plays and concerts were held. I knew where we were going now, and I knew why: Nigel.

This was my fault. I had to stop it. Somehow. Anyhow. Saltwater cures everything, Dad always says. It wouldn't cure whatever venom Edna had filled me with, but it would keep her from using me against him. I pushed to my feet, and tried to climb over the rail.

Jeff grabbed my arm and wrenched me back. "Where do you think you're going?" He shoved me to the deck.

I landed hard on my side, whimpering from the impact.

Edna tsked at me. "Now you just behave yourself." She smiled. "You wouldn't want anything to happen to Hailey, would you?" She stopped smiling. "Would you?"

"No." I whispered; helpless, horrified tears spilled down my cheeks.

"There's a good girl." She patted the seat beside her.

I sat where I was told, and she put her arm through mine, dabbing at my face with a tissue. I cringed, and had to fight hard not to shy away, or turn and claw her eyes out.

Jeff brought us to the dock, tossing lines to a waiting attendant to secure. Other boats lined the wooden pier, and people in their best dress stepped from their boats and were funneled inside. Cars streamed into the parking lot on land. There were hundreds of people all around.

I'd never felt so alone.

I should have been afraid.

I was too angry.

They led me toward the entrance, Edna clutching one arm, Jeff clamped on the other. His fingers clenched roughly, and he tapped Morse code on my skin: BE CHILL BABY

I followed his eyes, and caught a glimpse of red hair mostly gone to white; my father was here. He'd seen me. My legs nearly buckled. Jeff held me up.

Edna patted my arm sympathetically. "There, there. It'll all be done soon, and you'll have nothing more to worry about. It's a good thing you wore a dress, dear." She said as we were ushered up the stairs. "You fit right in. It is very pretty on you." Her claws clenched in my arm.

"Thank you." I murmured.

"That's right; manners matter." She patted my hand. She was wearing her ring. "Think what a lovely evening you have before you. You're quite fortunate, you know."

"Fortunate?" I sputtered.

"Yes," Edna smiled. "Why-"

"Bethany, darling!" Edith Alderson cut off Edna's words as she came rushing towards me, dressed in her customary white from head to toe, reaching to take my hands.

Edna tried to yank me away, but Edith was not a woman to have her will thwarted. She swooped in to kiss my cheeks - nearly elbowing Edna in the face in the process; I truly admired and respected that woman.

"Dr. Essex sends his regards." Edith whispered in my ear as she jabbed me in the side with something sharp.

I gasped, and felt warmth spread from the jab. The haze cleared from my eyes, and the pain in my joints melted away.

"I'd no idea you liked the opera!" Edith was extra gregarious to cover my reaction. She quickly pulled out what I guessed was a needle from my side - filled with something I understood was made by Nigel, and tucked it up her sleeve. My heart filled with hope. "You must join me in my box-"

"Some other time." Edna grimaced in what was supposed to be a smile, snagging my arm back from Edith.

"Another time would be lovely." I squeezed Edith's hand tight. "Thank you, Edith."

Edith bowed her head, and walked stiffly away.

Edna sniffed irritably, but I held my head a little higher, and saw my brother-in-law, Ray. He nodded almost imperceptibly from across the hall when he was sure I'd seen him, then went on ahead into the auditorium.

"Bethany - my muse!" Victor Powell charged at me; Jeff stiffened, gripping my arm tighter.

I had the distinct impression Victor wasn't a part of anyone's plans.

"Muse?" Jeff spat the word.

"Bethany is the inspiration for my latest book." Victor beamed, but he seemed more pleased with himself than with me. "I knew there had to be some horrible misunderstanding. That horrid little gremlin had the temerity to imply you were deliberately avoiding me!"

GET RID OF HIM. Jeff tapped.

"Gremlin?" I asked, ignoring Jeff. Two could play at that. I was going to draw this out as long as I could; it was annoying Edna. No win against her was too small for me.

"That *child*." Victor sniffed, saying the word as if it were a swear, or possibly a type of insect.

"Juliet?" Oh, good girl! "I'm so sorry, Victor, there was no way to contact you about the change-"

"Yes," Edna overrode me, digging her claws tight into my arm, warning me to be quiet. "Dear Bethany will be accompanying me to my private box." She very precisely enunciated the word 'private.'

"Ah," Victor didn't quite take the hint she was broadcasting. "Delighted to join you." He bowed to Edna; she gave a clipped squeak of indignation. "Be off." Victor ordered Jeff, trying to wrest my arm from his grip.

Jeff flared his eyes at me.

"Oh, Victor," I figured I'd pushed it as far as was safe. "I believe Edith was looking for you; something to do with your book launch-"

"Oh?" Victor looked clearly torn between rushing to her and staying with me. Momentarily. His mercenary side quickly won out. "I must speak with her at once!"

"It's too important not to." I encouraged him. "I think I see her." I pointed to the far end of the gallery.

"Ah, my muse!" Victor slobbered over my hand. "Such a considerate heart." He was off like a flash.

I scrubbed my hand on my dress, Jeff regained my arm, and we pressed on.

"He's not your type." Jeff sneered disgustedly at Victor's

retreating back.

"He's not like you." I noted.

"Exactly." Jeff shook his head. "You're not going to last."

I couldn't disagree.

"You're not even together." Jeff's nostrils flared. His eyes widened. "You're in love with Essex."

First Edith had said it, and now him? "You're delusional."

"You're–"

Edna cleared her throat irritably, and Jeff cut off whatever accusation he had been about to fling at me. He didn't have to say anything; his clenched jaw, blazing eyes, and death grip strangling my arm said enough. We made the rest of our way to the auditorium in strained silence, and started up the stairs to the balcony level.

My mother was coming down as we were going up. Her face was white with strain, and with fury. I looked at her with wide eyes, shaking my head to try and stop her from doing whatever she was intending.

Mom jabbed Edna in the face with her purse as she passed. Hard. "Oh, I'm so sorry!"

Edna reeled back, then struck out wildly with her fist, fang pointed out.

I stepped on the long hem of her dress, pinning Edna to the step she was on; her stubby little gnome arms couldn't reach.

Mom smiled viciously at me over top of Edna's gnomish head. "How careless of me." She continued on down the stairs.

I'd never felt so loved.

Edna turned a look of pure seething hatred on me. I raised an eyebrow, looking down on her from the step below her. She stuck her nose in the air, and led on. We stepped into Edna's private family box. Every seat was full, and with more than just

her family. My heart stopped beating.
I'd never felt so afraid.

15

Pawn Takes the Queen

"Nigel!" My voice came out shrill, high, my panic on full display. What was he doing here? How? Why? No! It wasn't safe! It-

"Bethany, darling." Nigel stood and bowed his head to me, smiling broadly. "So glad you could join me." He held out his hands.

I took one step forward, and was yanked back by Jeff.

"Let her go." Nigel ordered.

"What is this?" Edna demanded haughtily, looking around the box. The look turned into an accusatory one, leveled at Jeff.

He gave her a vicious self-satisfied smile. "Payback."

Movement in the box drew my gaze from Nigel, and from Jeff and Edna. We'd stepped into a battle, and the lines were clearly drawn, as were the guns: team Maestro on one side, team Sept on the other. But maybe it was a mistake to call them that? This wasn't teams - this was personal.

This was family.

Ryan Valentine stood to his full height, and did not look at all impressive for it. Sage, almost as wide as he was tall, stood behind him. Across the aisle, Jimmy and Frederic flanked Nigel, along with Evan Pope, and my brother Johnny. I smiled in relief at him.

He wasn't looking at me. I followed my brother's gaze to a point behind Sage, and the person I hadn't seen hidden behind his bulk: Spider.

Spider stood by Valentine, but whose side was he really on? I shoved that thought out of the way; there were far more pressing matters to attend to. Like the gun Valentine was aiming at Nigel.

That was not allowed.

I twisted out of Jeff's grip and pivoted, grabbing Edna by the hair with one hand, and gripping her hand wearing the poison-tipped ring with the other, holding the vile thing precariously close to her throat. I forced her in front of me - a tiny, screeching, gnome shaped shield - and placed myself between Nigel and Valentine.

I half expected Sage to shout 'Grandma;' it wouldn't have surprised me at all given the convoluted relationships I'd already teased apart today. Someone had to be eating all those cookies Edna was making. It would have fit. He didn't seem at all concerned about her, though.

Valentine sure did. "Let her go!"

"That's not very original." I said. "Or very likely. You're not getting something for nothing."

"What do you want?" He snarled.

"The truth." I said. "You owe it to your uncle."

Valentine's eyes narrowed. "What are you talking about?"

"Angelo." I looked into his eyes, and my theory fell apart.

Edna bucked. "Frederic did it!" She screeched. "Frederic killed him!"

"What are you talking about, you crazy old hag!" Frederic roared at her. "I loved my son! This was all Sept doing!" His voice cracked; Jimmy put his hand on his shoulder, supporting his brother. "I loved him."

All Sept? If he was blaming them, then he definitely wasn't the one in charge of them. Edna had lied. Why? Something was wrong. Something was missing. Someone? I needed to rebuild my theory, and fast. Valentine was in front of me; I started with him: "Tell me what happened Friday night."

"I can give you a reminder." Jeff stood perfectly still with his hands at his sides, staring at Valentine, daring him to twitch his gun toward him.

Valentine sneered at him. "Someone gave you a bad tip."

"Who?" I asked. Why, I wondered? A distraction. But for what?

What were the facts? Angelo had taken Nigel's car. Angelo was set to rise. You had to do something bold - something to get attention - to rise in the Sept. Stealing a car wouldn't cut it. But getting the man who owned it? Doing it in front of your top-tier cousin? If the cops hadn't shown up...

The Sept didn't look fondly on failure. It embarrassed them... If the cops hadn't been called, Angelo might have gotten away with it... Who told them? I looked at Jeff, his eyes locked on Valentine, and knew. It wasn't about them. It never was.

This was personal.

This was family.

I looked at the only man it could be about. The one I hadn't wanted to see. The one Angelo had wanted to impress. The one who blamed everyone but himself. The one who didn't brag. He lied. "This whole thing was a set up."

Pope shrugged. "You and your big mouth, Red."

"Evan?" Horror spread across Frederic's face.

Pope kept his eyes on me.

"You told me who Angelo was, and sent me..." I tilted my head, trying to see the angle, his angle. "You sent me out of the way." I said. "Why?"

"They let me get sent away!" Pope roared. "They left me to rot!"

"Evan, no!" Edna strained for him; I kept my grip fast.

He payed her no mind. "No help, no loyalty! Not from any of them!"

I felt ill. "He was just a kid-"

"He was a spoiled brat!" Pope shook his head. "I join the Sept, I get nothing but criticism; Angelo joins, he makes all the same mistakes I make and more, and he gets cheered on for it? It wasn't fair!"

"You set him up?" Johnny asked, trying to make sense of what he was hearing.

"You killed him." I said.

"He deserved it." Pope sneered.

"My muse!" Victor burst into the box, startling everyone. He saw all the guns suddenly pointed at him, and fainted.

Frederic recovered first, opened fire, and Pope went down. Valentine panicked, and shot Frederic; Frederic shot back and hit Sage, who keeled over and landed on Spider. Edna lurched out of my grip, running to Pope. Frederic toppled forward, and was caught by Jimmy. Nigel leaped over the chairs to try and help Jimmy stop Frederic's bleeding. Valentine stumbled into his seat, and stared at his gun in shock.

It all happened so fast.

I stood, stunned, in the midst of the carnage, and didn't know which way to turn.

Edna screamed, and turned on me. "It was supposed to be you! This is all your fault!" She ran at me, fangs first.

My legs were cooperating now. I kicked out hard and Edna staggered back, and tipped over the railing.

"No!" I lunged to grab her, but I was too late.

Screams erupted from below, and a stampede of patrons pushed toward the exits.

"Mother!" Valentine erupted from his seat, fumbling through his shock to point his gun at me.

Jeff didn't waste any time; he drew and fired before Valentine could get his gun half raised. Valentine wavered on his feet, then crumpled to the floor.

"It's alright! I'm here!" Victor announced, leaping to his feet in front of me, just in time to guard me. At least in his imagination.

Jimmy howled, the sound a wounded animal makes as his brother died.

My eyes found Nigel across the expanse of the box, white-faced, stricken, and coming toward me.

Jeff still had his gun out.

I didn't have a choice.

I wrapped my arms around Victor Powell's neck, and kissed him full on the mouth.

"Bethany?" Victor was stunned into stillness; as were Nigel and Jeff. For a moment. "My muse!" He tried to kiss me back.

Once was enough. And all I could take. I back-stepped and pivoted out of his reach. "I'm sorry, Victor. I don't know what came over me." I looked around, everywhere but at Nigel. "The shock..."

Victor looked thoroughly disappointed. He brushed at his suit, and straightened his tie. "I would have dealt with those miscreants."

I patted his arm sympathetically.

"No doubt, Victor." Nigel somehow managed a perfect deadpan. "No doubt."

Jeff looked sorely confused, and thoroughly disgusted. He shook his head, and holstered his gun, and went to help Johnny pry Spider out from under Sage.

"Bethany!" My father charged into the fray, followed by my mother, Ray, and Chief Patience.

Everyone froze.

Patience walked over to Valentine, looked down on him, and started to weep. "Thank you." She hugged Jeff.

He could do no wrong after this.

I ran to my father. Mom squeezed my hand, then went to look after Patience.

"Come on, Victor." Nigel put his arm around his shoulders, and directed him to the door. "I think we could both use a drink."

"If you're buying, I'm coming." Johnny included himself.

Nigel laughed. "More the merrier." That had a bitter note to it.

"Dr. Essex!" I couldn't let him go. He turned to look at me. So did Jeff. Darn it. "Thank you."

"My pleasure, Miss Knox." He bowed his head to me. "My very great pleasure."

The End

About the Author

Canadian author Stephanie Turner belongs to the Triple 'E' Club - an Easterner in Economic Exile. She lives with her husband and children in view of the Rocky Mountains, but longs for the shores of the Atlantic Ocean.

Until she can get home, she'll set her stories where her heart is, with occasional treks to drier regions, and the odd quest to galaxies far, far away.

When she's not writing, she can be found wandering through the local bird sanctuary, sketchbook in hand, or curled up in a comfy chair with a good book and a hot cup of tea.

Also by Stephanie Turner

Books in the Bethany Knox Private Investigator Series

Opportunity Knox

Bethany Knox Private Investigator #1

Billionaire scientist Nigel Essex is arrogant, obnoxious, and drop-dead gorgeous. But is he a murderer?

When Nigel Essex is accused of murdering his best friend, Bethany Knox of Opportunity Knox Private Investigators is hired to clear his name.

The trouble is, the jerk nearly ran over her with his boat - twice! - and she's pretty sure he's guilty.

If she doesn't get this right, an innocent man will go to jail, and a murderer will get off Scot-free.

How is she supposed to get past her first impression to find the truth?

Pretty in Poison

Bethany Knox Private Investigator #2

"Keep your nose out of business that doesn't concern you."

Did I just have a run in with Dr. Jekyll and Mr. Hyde?

When billionaire scientist Nigel Essex has suspicions about an employee stealing company secrets, he calls Bethany Knox of Opportunity Knox Private Investigators to investigate the matter.

The investigation takes a sinister turn when she finds the body in the lab.

Can she find who is behind this, and can she stop them before they do something worse?